GOODNIGHT TO THE RESCUE

I grabbed his wrists as he ran into me and fell backwards, feeling my neck strike the edge of the riverbank and the sharp drop-off right underneath it. I had damn little time to think, so my instincts and reflexes took over. I kicked my legs up, pushing the warrior up with them, I hoped. When the bottom part of his body went up, I pushed off the wrists I had hold of and he flipped over me and into the river.

I looked up quickly in the direction he had come from, only to see a handful of his friends coming toward me. . . . I was dead and I knew it. All I could do was cuss and pray. Still, I had the bowie knife at my side. I was reaching for it when I heard a half dozen shots ring out from the eastern bank of the river.

I rolled half over and immediately saw Charlie Goodnight and the Wilson brothers, each with a rifle in his hands, shooting at the charging warriors . . .

Books by Jim Miller

The 600 Mile Stretch
Rangers Reunited
Too Many Drifters
Hell with the Hide Off
The Long Rope
Rangers' Revenge

Published by POCKET BOOKS

6

THE EX-RANGERS

THE 600 MILE STRETCH

JIM MILLER

POCKET BOOKS

New York   London   Toronto   Sydney   Tokyo   Singapore

An Original Publication of POCKET BOOKS

POCKET BOOKS, a division of Simon & Schuster Inc.
1230 Avenue of the Americas, New York, NY 10020

Copyright © 1992 by James L. Collins

ISBN: 0-671-74824-6

First Pocket Books printing March 1992

10 9 8 7 6 5 4 3 2 1

POCKET and colophon are registered trademarks of
Simon & Schuster Inc.

Cover art by Garin Baker

Printed in the U.S.A.

THE
600 MILE
STRETCH

CHAPTER

★ · 1 · ★

Here you go, Miss Sarah Ann," Emmett said as he showed Wash's new wife the paint he'd tied up in front of our ranch house.

"Well, I'm flattered, Mr. Emmett," Sarah Ann said, a blush coming to her face as she took in the sight. Wash and Emmett and me had come across more than one paint pony while we'd broken the herd of mustangs that spring. We all knew that a horse of mixed color usually wasn't any good for much more than showing off. I'd mentioned giving one of the mounts to Sarah Ann, but Wash had balked at the idea, so I reckon it was Emmett who decided to go ahead with the gesture.

"Oh, it wasn't nothing, ma'am," Emmett said in what for him was pure modesty. "I give one of these animals to Greta just the other day. Likes 'em right well, she does."

Greta was Emmett's wife. She had been married to a man of German heritage who had gotten killed within the past year when some carpetbagger had come to Twin Rifles and tried bilking the townsfolk out of their money, not to mention robbing our bank. Emmett, a former sergeant in the Union army, had played a big part in foiling the bank robbery and bringing in the killers who had a hand in it. It was a shame that Greta and her family had gotten tossed into the middle of all of it and a bigger shame yet that she had lost her husband during the fracas. But that was the beginning of what turned out to be a romance between the big ex-sergeant and Greta, and six months later the two had been married.

After running a smooth hand along the paint's neck, Sarah Ann's expression suddenly became suspicious as she glanced from Emmett to Wash to me. "I don't suppose this is meant to be some kind of bribe, is it, Chance?" she asked me in a growing frown.

"Bribe? Why, of course not," I insisted with what I thought to be my straightest face. Actually, she had hit it right on the head, for it was Emmett and me who'd come up with the idea that giving the woman a gift might make it easier for her to let her husband go with us. "Now, what makes you say that, Sarah Ann?"

"Because it's the kind of thing you'd do, Chance Carston," she said flat out. No bones about it, this woman had caught me at it.

"Chance and Emmett didn't mean no harm, honey," Wash said, trying in a weak fashion to stand up for me. I almost had the notion he was afraid his wife might lose her temper and start sounding like Big John Porter, her daddy. And you didn't make Big

John any madder than you had to, at least not if you wanted to stay in one piece for long. I'd found out that Sarah Ann had a good deal of Big John's mad in her too when things didn't go her way. "He is a mighty pretty horse, you know."

"Oh, I know, Wash," Sarah Ann said, taking hold of my brother by the arm. "But do you really have to go on this silly cattle drive? Isn't it going to be awfully dangerous?"

"Why, shoot, ma'am, just living in this godforsaken land is dangerous," Emmett said, trying to reason with her, but only in the most careful of ways. "Besides, Chance and me'll make sure old Wash comes back safe and sound. You know that, Miss Sarah Ann."

"Now, Sarah Ann, we talked this over a while back and it was decided that Chance and me would break those mustangs for this Charlie Goodnight up to Fort Belknap and help him out on his drive to boot," Wash said, raising an eyebrow.

"I know," the woman he called his wife acknowledged in a sorrowful tone. "But I'm going to be so lonely while you're gone. And worried."

"Nonsense, ma'am," Emmett said, pushing his hat back on his head. "Why, Greta said she'd be in to town to visit you near every day."

"And Bell and Hood will be staying out here at the ranch to make sure everything's all right," I added, seeing only the slightest reassurance on the woman's face. Bell and Hood were two of Emmett's riding pards when he first rode into Twin Rifles. "Besides, Pa said him and that friend of his, old Dallas Bodeen, would be stopping by on a regular basis too."

I was tempted to add that one of the main reasons Wash, Emmett, and me had busted our git-up ends

3

this spring with those wild mustangs and agreed to go on this cattle drive was mostly because all three of us—Wash, Emmett, and me—were close to being flat broke. Wash and me had been trying to make a go of it breaking wild horses and selling them to the army ever since we'd come back from the war, but the army suddenly had enough mounts for a while, so the money had pretty much dried up right quick. That was when I'd met this Charlie Goodnight, who was talking about putting together a herd of cattle and trying to make a drive to a market later that spring. He was in need of horses and willing to pay top dollar for them if me and Wash could provide them for him. The trouble was he was needing close to sixty head for what he had in mind. That was how me and Emmett and Bell and Hood and my brother had managed to get saddle sore that spring. Hell, I figured we were lucky to wind up with just a bunch of tender bruises on various parts of our bodies instead of a whole mess of busted bones, which would have made this whole cattle drive thing a lot less appealing. I reckon you'd have to have busted a bone or two in your lifetime to appreciate what I'm talking about.

"Oh, I know the others will be by to check on me," Sarah Ann said, a look of sadness equal to the sound of her voice coming over her now. "It'd be hard not to expect your Papa not to make sure everything was all right with me." I knew what she was talking about, for the way Pa had been carrying on since Wash and Sarah Ann had gotten married, you'd have thought he was the one homesteading her instead of my younger brother. Took a real liking to Sarah Ann, Pa did. "It's just that I'm going to miss you so bad, Wash, that I don't think I'll be able to stand it." As she spoke, she ran a soft hand across Wash's face, then looked past him at me. A shy kind of smile appeared now as she added, "I imagine I'll even miss you, Chance, much as it pains me to say so."

You could have knocked me over with a feather! Mind you now, Sarah Ann had never been too fond of me or my way of handling things, which is head first. She's always liked the way Wash used his head before he'd use his fists to solve a situation. Me, well, I reckon if the man's close enough I'll take a swing at him . . . Being out of fistfight range, why, my natural instinct was to pull one of my Colts or my bowie knife to do him in. A long rifle was always my last resort after that. Get it done quick was always my way of thinking. You can pray over him later, if you like. So hearing this woman before me say she'd miss me, why, that was a shock my system wasn't prepared for.

"I won't even ask whether you'll miss me," Emmett said, only half in jest.

The man's comment tickled Sarah Ann. With a broadening smile, she said, "You'd better not, Sergeant Emmett, or it'll be me who's telling Greta about the other woman you want in your life."

"Oh, no, ma'am," Emmett said, a sudden urgency now about him. "Why, I don't think Greta could stand the news. No, ma'am." Wash and I grinned at one another, knowing full well that it would be Emmett who couldn't stand the news once that woman of his let her husband in on a dose of her German temper.

"Look, Sarah Ann, the fact of the matter is we're all needing money right now and this cattle drive and the horses we've been busting all spring are what's gonna put us back on our feet," Wash said, taking the woman in his arms and holding her dear to him as he spoke to her in his soft voice. Pushing her back at arm's length, there didn't seem to be anything else either one of them could say.

"What do you reckon it is, fear or the fact that they're married?" Emmett said, taking in the sight of the two speechless lovers.

"Look, Sarah Ann," I said after shaking my head. "What Emmett said is right. We'll make sure Wash comes back in one piece and breathing as regular as he is now. You're just gonna have to trust us to know what we're doing."

"He's right, girl," Emmett added. "You got a prime chance to be brave for the next month or two."

"Yes," Sarah Ann said in a low mournful voice. "I suppose so."

It was two weeks ago that Emmett had given that paint to Sarah Ann. We'd left a day or two afterward and had been on the trail with our sixty horses ever since, heading for Fort Belknap and Charlie Goodnight's herd of cattle. We'd been seeing cattle here and there in large numbers for the past hour or so and knew that we couldn't be far from Goodnight and his brands.

During our trek north, Emmett and me had our minds on the herd from dawn to dusk, but I knew for a fact that Wash had his mind on Sarah Ann. Hell, with that moon-eyed look about him, it couldn't have been anything else.

But then, that's what marriage does to a man, I reckon.

CHAPTER
★ 2 ★

We stopped at the Brazos River to let the mustangs water and searched out Charlie Goodnight, whose cattle seemed to be running loose all about the area.

"I reckon that'd be your man," Emmett said, spotting a man riding tall in the saddle and heading in our direction as the horses took their fill.

"What makes you say that?" I asked. It had been me who'd made the original deal with Goodnight to break a herd of wild horses and provide him with a remuda for the cattle driving trek he had in mind. And as far as I knew, I'd been the only one from Twin Rifles who'd ever laid eyes on Charlie Goodnight.

"He's got the look of a no-nonsense man," was Emmett's reply. "Kind of reminds me of you a mite,"

7

he added, although I wasn't sure whether the compliment was genuine or the occasional piece of flattery the ex-sergeant was known to hand out every once in a while. Or maybe just plain stretching the truth a mite. With Emmett you never could tell.

But Emmett was right. Even from the one time I'd dealt with him, it was easy to see that Charlie Goodnight said his words and meant every one of them, no bones about it. We'd sealed our deal with a handshake, which was good enough for both of us. I reckon Emmett was right if he thought Goodnight was my kind of man, for that indeed he was. Sometimes riding a horse will throw off what a man really looks like as far as his true stature. But I knew for a fact that Charlie Goodnight was over six feet tall, just like me, and was likely somewhere near my age, in his thirties. Like me he'd spent some time with the Texas Rangers and, if that was any indication, probably knew a good deal of this land as though it were the back of his hand. Aside from that he was sporting a beard on his face that was showing signs of going to gray.

"Glad you could make it, Carston," Goodnight said as he pulled his mount to a halt and took in the horses as they drank. "Looks like some fine mustangs." Emmett had been right about the man being no-nonsense, for even as he spoke his eyes were wandering over our mustangs, obviously eyeing the ones he thought would make the best trail horses.

"Sure took long enough," Emmett said, referring to the amount of time we'd spent in breaking the wild horses this spring, I thought.

"Just where is it you plan on taking all these cattle you've got spread out all over the place?" Wash asked after I'd introduced Emmett and my brother to Goodnight.

8

"Didn't your brother tell you? We'll be going to Fort Sumner in the New Mexican Territory to sell the better part of the herd," Goodnight said by way of explanation.

"I see," Wash said and gave me a sidelong glance, wondering why I hadn't told him more than I had. I knew that someday we'd get around to discussing that matter.

"Emmett's the best man I know of with a horse," I said to Goodnight. "I'd suggest letting him run the remuda on this drive of yours."

"Fine," Goodnight said. To Emmett he added, "I reckon we'll have some mighty fine cow horses by the time this drive is over with." I knew by the strict tone of the man's voice that he hadn't just been speaking idle thoughts, but was giving an order to Emmett. When Emmett gave me a side glance that said he knew what the man had said and what it had implied, I was sure he would ask Goodnight if he cared to dance. But for some strange reason, Emmett, who would fight at the drop of a hat at any other time, took a look at Wash beside me and must have run the thought through his mind before speaking.

"I'll do my best," was all Emmett said in reply. It left me wondering if Emmett wasn't taking this promise we'd made to Sarah Ann to keep Wash in good condition a mite too serious. After all, Emmett had seen Wash fight as much as I had in the last year or so and knew good and damn well that my brother, although a tad shorter and skinnier than me, did better than average at holding his own in any kind of a fight, take your pick.

We got the horses settled down and were invited into Goodnight's camp afterward. As we dismounted, Emmett squinted at the contraption he saw before him, which looked like it had once been a government wagon of sorts.

"Now, what in the devil is that?" he asked Goodnight.

"Oh that's a little invention of my own for this drive," Goodnight said and went on to explain just what purpose it served.

It had indeed once been a government wagon, but had now been totally redesigned to fit Charlie Goodnight's needs. The wagon had been entirely rebuilt with the toughest wood available, seasoned· bois d'arc. Rather than the usual wood, the axles were now made of iron, and in place of a tar bucket there was now a can of tallow to use in its greasing. The wagon would carry not only the food but the bedroll of every man on the drive, as well as any excess equipment that might be carried along; things like a flour box, a coffee grinder, and a water barrel. The back end of the wagon had a hinged lid that could be let down on a swinging leg to form a cook's worktable of sorts. Once swung down, it made available to the eye what Goodnight called a chuck box, which was fitted with compartments to hold the various provisions and utensils the cook would be taking along. A low leather sling under the wagon would carry wood and dried buffalo chips for the fire.

"That there wagon is gonna carry our chuck on this drive," he continued. Charlie Goodnight, it appeared, had invented what he called a "chuck wagon."

We dismounted and Charlie Goodnight found some tin cups and grabbed hold of a larger than normal size coffeepot sitting aside the fire and poured us all some of the hot stuff. I got the impression that at least the man wouldn't turn you away from the fire without a cup of coffee in your belly. No one who'd lived on this frontier for any length of time would. Life was just too hard and short.

"I hear there's a lot of fellas making their way north to those Missouri railheads with their mavericks," Wash said, taking a sip of his coffee. "Why are you heading over New Mexico way?"

A half smile appeared on Goodnight's face. "Actually, it's pretty simple, Carston."

"If we're gonna be working together, you can call me Wash," my brother said. Always the friendly sort, he was. Tossing a thumb in my direction, he added, "You'll find my brother goes by the handle of Chance."

Charlie Goodnight nodded in silence, as though that alone were enough to assure the man he would remember our first names from now on. Once that was out of the way, he continued to answer my brother's question.

"I'm heading for Fort Sumner because there's a whole lot of them fellas making their way north to them railheads in Missouri," he said. Wash blushed a mite, realizing, I thought, that he'd really answered his own question in asking it. "Missouri ain't the only market for cattle, you know. There's an Indian reservation or two over New Mexico way that's in need of cattle to feed their Indians. I checked them out and signed a contract to deliver as many as I could to them this summer."

I swallowed the rest of my coffee, which wasn't bad at all, and refilled the cup halfway.

"You know, Charlie," I said to the man, taking a chance on using his first name, "I was doing some thinking on that on the way up here. Ain't never been no cattle sent in that direction that I can recall hearing of."

"That's right," Charlie Goodnight replied, apparently not taking offense at the liberties I'd taken in using his first name. "Hasn't been done before that I know of either."

"That's what I thought."

Actually, I'd done a lot more thinking than that. I knew, for example, that there had been some cattle drives before the war that headed over into Louisiana. Why, there was even one fellow who'd driven a small herd of cattle all the way to that fancy east coast town, New York City. Paraded his cattle right down Broadway, from what Pa had told me. And I knew that there was a shortage of beef back east now that the war was over. The idea of making ten, fifteen, even twenty dollars a head off of cattle that you could round up for nothing was real appealing to many a man in Texas, especially those who were next to penniless, which was a good share of the population, I was willing to bet. So rounding up a bunch of stray long-horned cattle and taking them to market wasn't out of the realm of reason at all. But that wasn't what had been bothering me on our way to Charlie Goodnight's outfit, and I finally decided to get it off my mind. After all, the man who could finally answer my question was standing right before me now.

"Tell me something, Charlie," I said, sipping my steaming cup of coffee.

"If I can."

"Just how did you plan on getting these longhorns to Fort Sumner? You got a particular path mapped out in your mind?" I asked.

Charlie Goodnight picked up a piece of thin deadwood and proceeded to draw a map in the dirt before us. He started with the letter Y, the fork of which pointed to the west. "Those forks are the Upper and

Lower Concho Rivers," he said by way of explanation. "We'll cross both of them, heading south out of Belknap when we leave."

"I see."

His expression had taken on a deadly serious nature now as he took in Emmett, Wash, and me. I almost got the impression he didn't want to talk about what he was going to say next. "The hardest part of our trek comes next, as we head for the Pecos River." He now reached out before him and drew a jagged line about three feet from the first part of his dirt map. "I figure from here to here is a hundred miles," he finally said as he pointed first to the Concho Rivers and then to the jagged line, which I could only imagine was to indicate the Pecos River. If he was looking for concern on our faces, he likely saw just that as he looked us over now.

"Well, Charlie, you're gonna have to tell me just what it is we're getting ourselves into here," I said. "Hell, I never did travel that far west, not by the Pecos country, anyway. And I've been away for the better part of four years, so if I knew once, I'd likely forget about it by now."

As Grandma once put it, Charlie let the cat out of the bag.

"We'll be taking this herd—and your horses—across a stretch of land they call the Llano Estacado," he said in a slow, deliberate way. "They call it the Staked Plains."

I thought I felt some coffee spill from my cup onto my hand, and when I looked down I saw that was exactly what I'd done. But you know something? I don't think it even burned me, hot as that coffee was. Hell, it couldn't have. The chill that was running through my body now was colder than any winter

13

blizzard I could remember sitting through. And in this land, that's saying something.

The Llano Estacado.

Most of the time I'd spent as a Texas Ranger before the war I'd spent roaming up north around the Indian Territory and down south of the border some, and even into some of the grasslands of eastern Texas. But I'd never had much business to take care of in the western part of Texas, never had any outlaws to chase that far west. One of the few times I'd given it much thought, I'd come to the conclusion that maybe what they said about there being no God or Law west of the Pecos . . . well, maybe they were right. From what I'd heard the whole western part of Texas was a land controlled by the Kwahadi band of the Comanche Indian nation. The Kwahadi were rumored to be the fiercest of all the Comanches and if that were true so be it. We'd had enough trouble just handling the lesser known bands in our part of southern Texas; I had no inclination to see if I could take on the Kwahadi. Heck, there were days I wasn't even sure I was up to the heathens who invaded our own backyard on occasion.

Not that I was totally ignorant of what the Llano Estacado was like, for I'd known men who'd survived the area and eagerly bragged about it. According to Pa, who'd been just about everywhere to hear him tell it, the Staked Plains—*Llano Estacado* is the literal Spanish translation of "Staked Plains"—was one of the most perfect plains regions in the world. For the most part it is a high plateau, one giant irregularly shaped mesa that looks like the Almighty just planted it there when He was through making the world and, on the seventh day, found He had a big flat piece of stony area left over. Now you've got to remember that when I use the word giant to describe this chunk of land, I'm not exaggerating one bit! That plateau extends from the central western part of Texas northward over most of the Panhandle of Texas and westward into the eastern part of what they were calling New Mexico.

Apparently, the Llano is more clearly defined on the east and west sides than anywhere else. Its western boundary pretty much follows the Pecos River, which stretches out a far piece, from what I'm told. The eastern boundary is more a clifflike ledge that appears out of nowhere. I'd never been to the Rocky Mountains, where Pa had spent much of his youth as a trapper, and could only imagine his comparison of the two structures when he said, "All of a sudden they're there!" I reckon they sort of spring on you like a Comanche war party. Now *that* was something I'd had a lot of experience with!

As vast and scary as the area and its descriptions might be to some, what stuck in my mind, and what had sent the chills running down my spine, was the all too dominant fact that *there wasn't a drop of water on that whole parched piece of rock!*

"I've heard stories of that place," I said.

"So I gather," Charlie Goodnight said with a crooked smile about him as he took in the coffee I'd spilled on my hand. "It's about the same reaction I get from most when I tell 'em I'm fixing to blaze a trail across a straight piece of flat rock."

I thought I saw a bit of concern on the faces of Emmett and Wash, two men I'd grown to have at least a grudging respect for of late. Wash was my brother and we'd had our share of differences over the years, but ever since we'd come back from the war we seemed to have an understanding between us. It was almost as though life had become suddenly more serious and we had little or no time to horse around. As for Emmett, well, he was a former sergeant in the Union army, which was just as good as being a brother to me, especially since I'd been a sergeant too.

"Here you go," Charlie Goodnight said as he re-filled my coffee cup. "They tell me this stuff will settle your nerves," he added, with that hint of a grin to his face as he spoke.

CHAPTER
★ 3 ★

When we arrived, Charlie Goodnight was in the process of hiring the hands he figured he'd need for this trail drive he was putting together. One of the men who'd joined him was a fellow he'd worked with before, a man by the name of "One-Armed" Bill Wilson. Not that the man had but one arm, you understand. It was just that his left arm had been brought up lame one way or another, so his right arm was the one he used most, thus the nickname One-Armed Bill. There are some things you flat out don't ask a man, and how he come by a stove-up limb is one of them. Not unless you're looking for an early grave, that is. And if Bill Wilson wasn't holding conventions about how his arm got stove up, well, hoss, I wasn't looking for a debate either.

One of the reasons I wasn't asking was because Charlie Goodnight, who'd worked with One-Armed Bill before, said that the man was good when trouble came about. Managed to be in trouble a good deal of his life, from what I understand. Fact of the matter was, One-Armed Bill Wilson had been in a good deal of trouble up Jacksboro way when Goodnight had gotten hold of him about coming along on this drive of his. I never was clear on how it all came about, but this Wilson character had gotten into some kind of trouble with a group of unsavory yahoos who'd taken him prisoner. According to Charlie Goodnight, when word of Wilson's difficulty came down, Charlie had sent a rider with a message for Wilson. Goodnight had advised Wilson to buy all the whiskey his money could get and pretend to drink but stay sober, if you know what I mean. Wilson did, and sure enough, his escorts had discovered his whiskey and taken on the chore of disposing of all that liquor so there wasn't a drop left between them. By the time that happened they were dead drunk, and One-Armed Bill Wilson swung his spurs into his mount and lit a shuck out of that country and straight for Goodnight's camp. So far no one had been seen coming after him.

It was my understanding that Charlie Goodnight put a lot of faith in this Wilson, and it was his lash-up, so that was fine with me. Besides, the way I was looking at the whole situation, we were going to be needing not only horses with a lot of bottom to them but some damn good men as well before this little trek was over.

"Chance, how'd you like to do some riding with me?" Charlie Goodnight asked as he approached Emmett, Wash, and me the morning after we'd arrived in camp. The three of us were still new in camp and staying pretty much to ourselves until we'd gotten to know the other men on the drive. I'd counted upwards of a dozen and a half since I'd been in camp, a number that didn't surprise me. The more time passed, the more folks seemed to be doing in this land. Trouble was they were having to use more men to do it with. Now, back when I was a ranger, why, if there was one riot, they sent one ranger . . .

I turned my thoughts back to Charlie Goodnight's question. "What is it you got in mind?"

"Those fellers that had Wilson called themselves Unionists," he said, which didn't do a hell of a lot by way of explanation. "Turns out they might have some of our cattle." Charlie Goodnight swallowed the rest of his coffee, a sour look taking over his face, a look I knew had nothing to do with the taste of the black stuff. "I mean to get 'em back," he growled.

There has always been something about a good fight that gets me excited, if you know what I mean. Pa labeled me a troublemaker back in my youth, but I've always thought it was the love of a good fight that'd gotten me into most of my fandangos, or whatever you want to call them. Guns, knives, fists—you take your pick—offer me a good one and I'll fight at the drop of a hat. And if you don't believe me, just ask Pa. I've heard him complain about it enough over the years to know how much he believes in what he says. I couldn't tell you whether it was that slightly crazy look in Charlie Goodnight's eye or the way he said "I mean to get 'em back" that told me I'd be in a good foofaraw before the day was over. I didn't hesitate in volunteering my services at all.

"Charlie, you've got yourself a saddle pard," I said in what I'm sure was an eager manner. "What about Emmett and Wash?" I added, always being one who wanted to give his brother and best friend a chance to get in on a good fight.

"No, I've got other designs for them," he replied. He took in Emmett and Wash when he spoke next. To Emmett he said, "If you're as good with horses as Chance says, you've still got a hell of a job cut out for you, mister. I'm gonna assign a man by the name of Cimarron to help you with the horses." To Wash, he said, "I'm figuring that you know Emmett better than I do, so I want you to help this new man out the best you can. You know, explain whatever it is your friend can't get across to him. It's my understanding that Emmett here's a Yankee sergeant, and I ain't seen a Yankee yet who could speak Mexican or Spanish or anything close to it. So you translate whatever needs to be said and pitch in where it's needed. You two got that?"

"Yes, sir," Emmett and Wash said in unison.

Something didn't seem all that right with what I'd just heard. It bothered me as I saddled my mount and readied to ride with Goodnight and two or three others from camp. By the time we'd left the camp, it was really bothering me.

"Tell me something, Charlie," I said as we rode out of camp a short time later.

"If I can."

"I got the impression you were awful cautious back there about taking Emmett and Wash along with us," I said, tossing a thumb over my shoulder. "Nothing personal, you understand, but do you mind telling me why you don't want them along? They're good men. I know because I've fought beside both of them."

I knew Charlie Goodnight wasn't one of those men who'd deliberately go looking for trouble and I thought I saw that kind of caution come over his face now as he conjured up his words. He'd get along fine with Pa, I thought, who was big on thinking before acting most times. I may have been sure about Goodnight, but I had a notion he wasn't yet too sure about me, if you get my drift.

"Listen, Chance, you ain't one of them fellers who'll start a feud over something that's said about his family, are you?" he finally spit out.

"I reckon that depends on what it is you're saying about my family, Charlie," I said, suddenly feeling a tenseness engulf my body.

"Well, it's like this, friend," he continued. "I ain't saying your brother and that Emmett feller ain't got no sand, not at all."

"Then what is it?" I didn't know whether or not Goodnight saw my fist squeezing into a ball or not, nor did I care. If the man wanted to go to war, then by God I'd oblige him!

It turned out he didn't. A crooked sort of smile crept over his face now as he pushed his hat back on his head. "It's just that your brother, why, he reminds me of one of them meek fellers who's supposed to inherit the earth."

Then I knew what it was he was getting at, thought I knew why he'd done what he did. The tautness I'd felt in my muscles was now gone, my fist no longer a tightly wound ball. Charlie Goodnight wasn't concerned about Wash or Emmett and whether they could fight if called upon. It wasn't that at all.

"I reckon Wash is a mite worried about Sarah Ann," I said. "He just got married a while back and he's probably worried about his woman and whether she's all right."

"Oh," Goodnight said, as though that explained it all. "I thought I was gonna have to remind him that

21

the meek ain't gonna inherit nothing west of St. Louis. Not in this land, anyway."

I smiled. "Ain't that the damn truth." Charlie Goodnight and me, why, we understood more of each other than we thought. This world was full of fussing and fighting and there wasn't no two ways about it, as far as I was concerned. As for the meek, well, if they inherit the earth like the Good Book says, I figure they'll have one hell of a time keeping it! "What about Emmett?"

"Well, hoss, I got the notion he was looking to mother that brother of yours while he's on that drive. Looks about as worried too," Charlie said. The hint of a smile crept into his face again, as he added, "Maybe if we keep the two of 'em together for a while, they'll calm down."

I agreed and we rode on.

The fellows who called themselves Unionists weren't anything new. Like the Red Legs and Jayhawkers who preceded them before the war, they were a band of men using what seemed like a patriotic label to some but what was really a front for what could only be termed illegal activities. Texas had been a dangerous place to hang anything with the Union label on it during the war, so these Jacksboro birds had fled to the sanctuary of southern Kansas during the War Between the States. When the fighting was over, they stole horses from the friendly Jayhawkers and rode back to Texas where, in favor with federal authorities, they began wreaking vengeance on the Texans who had run them out. Charlie Goodnight called them "alleged Unionists," and I couldn't say as I blamed him. Hell, these yahoos were neither loyal nor honest, if the information gathered was accurate.

It seemed they'd taken to the indiscriminate gathering of cattle, throwing a herd together on a place called Bean's Prairie, located east of Jacksboro. It was there we were headed and there Charlie Goodnight felt certain we'd find some of his missing cattle.

When we came upon a herd of cattle, there looked to be about a thousand or so of them roaming the range. We split up and circled the herd in opposite directions, looking for the brands Charlie Goodnight was fixing to push along with his own cattle.

"What's your find?" Goodnight asked One-Armed Bill Wilson, who'd circled the far side of the herd, when we met.

"I count twenty, maybe thirty head that's ours," he said.

"Same here," Charlie said, a scowl forming on his forehead. "I'd gauge around seventy-five in all." That was as far as any discussion went. When Charlie pulled out his six-gun and checked his loads, I followed suit and did the same. "Wilson, take these men and cut our cattle out. All of 'em. Chance, you come with me. We're gonna find whoever it is that's in charge of this herd."

I nodded and tugged on the reins of my mount, riding right beside Charlie Goodnight as we headed for a gathering of men who looked like they were about to change money between them.

"Looks like we got here just in time," I commented to Charlie, but he didn't seem to be interested in that.

Instead, he gave me a short glance and asked, "You did say you was a ranger once upon a time, didn't you?"

"That's a fact," I replied. If he was wanting to know if I'd stand beside him instead of behind him, I reckon the sure knowledge that I'd been a ranger during my lifetime was enough of a verification for the man. You don't last long in the Texas Rangers if you can't hold your own, hoss.

The fellow handing out the money looked more like a banker than any kind of working man. He wore a dark broadcloth suit with a hat that, although it matched the rest of his garb, barely fit his balding head. The man beside him wasn't any bigger, but he looked like he could hold his own a sight better than Mr. Money Man. I figured the companion for being the cowhand who was about to take charge of the herd, if indeed they were buying the herd.

Charlie Goodnight put a stop to that right quick.

"I don't know if you want to hand over that kind of money to the man you're fixing to pay it to," he said as we neared the two. I noticed that the man being paid the money had a half dozen amigos backing him up. I undid the thong on my Colt army model .44 and loosened the weapon in its holster, just to let them know I was ready to argue any old way they wanted to.

"And who might you be?" the Money Man asked in a bit of a stubborn way. These businessmen never do like having an important transaction interrupted.

"Name's Charlie Goodnight. Out yonder's some of my men. They're cutting my cattle out of this herd," Charlie added as though it were nothing.

Mr. Money Man was taken aback, either at Charlie's boldness or what he'd just said. Or maybe both. "Why, you can't do that! That's stealing!" the man blurted out in anger, nearly dropping the money left in his hand. I wondered if he knew that the man he was paying it to was just as likely to grab it out of his hand at that moment. He had a greedy look about him, which told me a lot.

"Don't tell me I can't, mister, because I'm doing it right now. As for stealing, you'd better talk to this yahoo about that particular line of work. I don't figure taking my own cattle back is anything close to stealing." The fire was back in Charlie's eyes, or perhaps it had never left. He'd started out real neighborly, but flat set the record straight when the suited-up banker type tried getting tough. By God, he was my kind of man, old Charlie Goodnight!

"Is that right, Mr. Fredericks?" the Money Man asked, his voice shifting from one of anger to one of astonishment. "Did you steal this man's cattle?"

"Hell no! Don't listen to him! Why, he's a liar, can't you see?" the man calling himself Fredericks said.

"Calling a man a liar is a poor choice of words, mister," I said in a hard even tone. "I've known more than one man who died with those words on his lips."

"If you're smart, you'll hang on to that money and find a different investment, mister," Charlie said to the Money Man, "for I'm not selling my cattle. Not here, anyway. And if you don't believe me, you just have your man check those longhorns my men are cutting out and he'll find three different brands that belong to my herd." Here Charlie Goodnight named the three brands. Upon hearing it, the working hand with the Money Man climbed on his horse and did exactly what Charlie had suggested.

In the meantime, the Money Man grabbed his fistful of dollars back and waited a few minutes until his companion returned. Fredericks, or whatever his name was, didn't like that one bit, a look of frustration working its way across his face as he waited for what he must have known in his heart would be the cowhand's news upon his return.

"It's just like he said, Mr. Harris," the cowhand said as he reined in his horse. "Looks to me like you been dealing with a snake," he said, casting an evil eye toward Fredericks and his men. "Ain't no telling how many of the rest are stolen either. You ask me, the man's right. We need to find another investment."

"What'd you two say your names were?" Fredericks asked in as mean a tone as I would have expected from such a man.

"Charlie Goodnight."

"And Chance Carston. Why do you ask?" I said.

A sneer appeared on his lips now. "I want to be able to get the names right when I dig your graves."

"I'd watch that kind of talk, mister," Charlie said. "I never did take kindly to threats."

"He's right, Fredericks," I added with a sneer of my own. "You try something like that and you could find yourself full of enough lead to make it worth hiring someone to dig it out of you."

People like Fredericks don't like being talked down to like that, but then you never can expect much better from horse and cattle thieves.

"I meant what I said, Goodnight!" Fredericks said to our backs and we slowly wheeled our mounts around and pointed them toward One-Armed Bill Wilson and the rest of Goodnight's men, who now had the longhorns under control and were slowly moving out toward Fort Belknap.

Charlie Goodnight pulled his mount to a halt and turned around in the saddle so he was talking to Fredericks over his shoulder.

"You'll find me down at Fort Belknap, Fredericks," he said. "Tell you what. You figure out who it is you don't need in your crew no more and you send 'em down after me."

"Why's that?" Fredericks asked, a bit confused at Charlie's words.

With a growl, Charlie replied, "Because when I get through with 'em, *they ain't coming back!*"

If Fredericks didn't have any idea who he was tangling with when we'd first rode up to his camp, he sure did now!

CHAPTER

★ 4 ★

Whether they knew it or not, Wash and Emmett had one of the more important jobs to perform on this so-called trail drive. I reckon what it all came down to was the fact that, as appealing as it was to get these longhorns to a market and get paid big money for them—Charlie Goodnight said they were willing to pay upwards of eight to sixteen cents a pound for these mangy critters, a thought that staggered my imagination and made me wish I was better with figures than I was—you couldn't do it worth a damn unless you had a good horse underneath you. It was amazing what you had to learn about herding a bunch of stubborn cattle along a trail that wasn't even broken yet, purely amazing. But Charlie Goodnight seemed to know what he was doing, so I wasn't about to say nothing but "Yes, sir" to him when he wanted something done around the camp.

It was the day after our run-in with Fredericks and his Unionists that I spent the better part of the day working with Emmett, Wash, and also their new *compadre*. Cimarron was a young fellow I gauged to be about twenty. You never can tell the age of a body too accurately out here, so it was hard telling for sure. Let's just say he was younger than me, likely around Wash's age, probably not younger. For the most part he was a quiet type, not speaking unless he was spoken to first but always doing what he was told without a fuss. Like most Mexicans, he had black hair and equally black eyes and was of average height, which made him a good deal shorter than me, Wash, and Emmett. Still, his height, or lack of it, didn't seem to stop him from doing his job. Like Pa told us way back when, "It ain't what you got but how you use it." I had a notion young Cimarron had learned how to put that to use long ago. He was also good with horses, even the randy bunch of mustangs we'd brought up the trail.

A *remuda* was what Emmett was put in charge of handling for this drive. It's a Spanish word meaning "to exchange." But for all intents and purposes, it would mean a group of extra horses that were kept for the men on this drive, horses that were not under saddle at the time.

"I'm counting on these horses being good ones, boys," Charlie said to the four of us that morning before taking off to perform other duties. "You give the men on this drive a good string of horses and I guarantee you they'll be able to handle most any trouble comes along."

"And if they're not?" I asked, curious as to what else he had to say.

Charlie ran a thoughtful hand across his bearded face, that hint of a smile coming to him as he spoke now. "You cut these fellers a bunch of plugs and they damn sure ain't gonna be working with us for long."

"I see." The words were self-explanatory.

According to Charlie, each of the eighteen men on the drive would have a minimum of three horses. Driving a herd of cattle was going to be pretty tough on the horses, so a man would be allotted one horse for the morning and one for the afternoon of each day, along with a night horse to stand guard on the herd. These horses wouldn't be used simply for keeping their riders off the ground. Charlie was expecting Emmett to be able to pick out the ones that would make good rope horses, good cutting horses, and even good river horses.

"Lordy!" was all Emmett could mutter once he'd heard Goodnight's requirements of the horses he'd be using. "As much as you're looking for from these mustangs, why, it sounds like you're wanting 'em to be able to dance a two-step by the time this drive's over!"

With a straight face, Charlie said, "If you can manage it, that would be fine."

Most men wound up picking and choosing among the remuda for the horses they wanted. I reckon it worked better that way. You might as well get along with the horse you were going to be riding as opposed to fighting him all the time. It would be hard enough putting up with this rowdy bunch of cattle, let alone having to fight your mount! The picking was done by seniority, the foreman getting first choice, for example. And if a rider was to quit or get fired, why, the horses in his string wouldn't be used again until he either came back or another rider was hired to take his place.

When I'd first met Charlie Goodnight and he'd approached me about furnishing horses for his trail drive, he'd made sure and impressed upon me the fact that he didn't want any horses younger than four years old. All the horses had to be geldings too. He assured me that they would ultimately make the best cow horses. Nor did he want any mares in his remuda. When I asked him how come, he said, "Mares is like female sisters. Always wanting to go someplace." He paused a few seconds in that way he had, and added, "And there's usually some fella willing to court 'em too." The idea being that stallions and mares simply didn't mix, having those strong kinds of feelings for one another. I could see what he was driving at. It was better to have a gelding, a horse with a lot of time on his hands, so to speak, to get the work done. There were far less distractions too, if you see what I'm getting at.

"Does he know how long it'd take to train these hosses to do all he wants?" Emmett asked in frustration after Goodnight walked off to leave us to our work. "Why, under normal circumstances, it'd take a good three years to get all that he wants done! Three goddamn years! Now I ask you, Chance, do I look like a saint? Do I look like some miracle worker?"

"Emmett, ugly as you are, I could never take you for being some kind of holy man," I said in reply. Of course, I made sure I was out of his reach when I said what I did. Emmett wasn't any too pleased with what he'd been handed as an assignment for this trail drive.

One of the things Cimarron turned out to be good at was using a rope. Now, hoss, roping a horse from a remuda was something that could only be described as a science, something you learn from experience. And Cimarron had that.

31

The figuring that went through the roper's mind wasn't anything you'd find on a fancy blackboard, I guarantee you that. He had to conjure up the direction of the wind, its rate of speed, and just how far astray his rope would be carried while he sent it sailing through the air, not to mention the distance between him and the horse he was aiming for.

"Good man," I said to him when he'd roped two of the mustangs and made it look like easy work. "You're gonna work out fine," I added and slapped him on the back as though he were a personal friend.

"Gracias, Señor Chance," he replied with an appreciative smile. I figured I was on my way to making a friend.

Wash, on the other hand, I was about ready to go to war with. He didn't seem to be able to do anything right, still acting like he was coming up the trail, as though something was bothering him deep within that he couldn't shake. Cimarron had taken to showing him how to rope a mustang, but my brother didn't seem to be able to do it worth squat, and I knew he was better with a rope than that!

"Let's take a break, Wash," I said later in the morning. "I could use some coffee and you look like you could too." We left Emmett and Cimarron to work together, which the two men did quite well, I thought. After handing my brother a cup of the black stuff, I squatted down in the shade, but he just stood there and stared off into the distance.

"Whatever it is you're looking for, I doubt you'll find it out there," I said in as brotherly a fashion as I knew how.

"Now, what's that supposed to mean?" From the tone of his voice, it was plain to see that Wash wasn't looking for any brotherly love. Me, I could live with that. Hell, most times I preferred it.

"It means you're moving but you ain't *doing* nothing out there, Wash," I said with a growl so he'd know I meant business. "It means you got something on your mind when it shouldn't be. It means if you don't get rid of it pretty damn soon, you could wind up costing someone his life on this drive, even your own." I can't say as I was ever anything less than truthful with my brother. But Wash wasn't looking for truth. Not today.

He hit me. Hard.

I staggered back, like I'd done a hundred times before when taking on my younger brother. It wasn't that he hit me that bothered me so much as the fact that he'd knocked a full cup of coffee out of my hand in the doing of it. He was swinging a big roundhouse punch at me a second time when my arm caught it and blocked it. I grabbed the arm he'd been making his swing with and pulled it toward me, bringing my left fist up into his brisket. The blow knocked the wind out of him and this time it was Wash who staggered some as he regained his senses.

"You don't want to do this, brother," I growled at him, hoping he would stop. Suddenly, it seemed as though he was looking for a fight, looking for an outlet for whatever demons were tormenting him at the moment. Besides, he was my brother and I'd whipped his ass more than once in my lifetime, left him good and bloodied, if memory served me correct.

He didn't hear my words. He swung at me twice more and I blocked him twice more, pushing him away as though he were some pest I had no desire to fight with. Then he made another quick move—Wash had always been quick, I'll give him that—and grabbed me by the throat with one hand and hit me hard in the face with the other until I was almost senseless.

There was blood coming out of the side of my mouth and, damn it, I was getting tired of toying with this young cub! I pulled the same tactic on him as he had me, grabbing his throat with one big hand and repeatedly smashing my other fist into his mouth until I imagined he felt as senseless, or close to it, as I had.

"That's enough!"

The voice was hard and tense and it belonged to Charlie Goodnight. I looked about and saw that there had been a gathering of some of the crew to watch us as Wash and I battered one another. I thought we should be in a saloon instead of in the middle of a camp outdoors. Charlie Goodnight sat as tall and straight as an arrow atop his mount as I'd ever seen him. But he wasn't finding anything funny or entertaining in the fandango Wash and I had just gone through. We both looked at him, looked at the crowd.

"Now, boys, you listen to me," Charlie said in a commanding voice that took in not just my brother and me but the whole camp. "There'll be no fighting in this camp or on this drive, and I mean from now until the day you get paid."

"But boss, they're brothers," Emmett said, trying to step in on our behalf, I thought. "Just having a misunderstanding . . . or something."

"I don't care if it's Jesus Christ and Judas Iscariot fighting it out like they should have in the first place!" Charlie roared. "You two or anyone else wants to fight, you can draw your pay and pack your bedroll, 'cause I got no use for you. Understand?" There were some murmurs among the hands that were supposed to sound like "yes" I reckon. "Good. Now get back to work. You're burning daylight!"

Wash walked off in silence, giving me a harsh look as he did. I still didn't know what it was that was eating him.

On the other hand, I thought I'd found out a bit more about Charlie Goodnight.

CHAPTER

★ 5 ★

Come 'n get it afore I throw it out!"

The cook's morning greeting was almost getting to be tolerable as his angry voice brought the world back to me. It had been that way the last few days after we'd returned from our stolen cattle roundup and confrontation with Fredericks, the so-called Unionist.

"Damn, but you're loud, Cookie," I said as I rolled out of my blankets, sloshed on my hat, and shook out my boots. I ain't seen a man yet who didn't put his hat on his noggin then shake out his boots in the early hours of the morning. After I made sure there weren't any tarantulas in my foot gear, I started feeling around in the dark for where I thought I'd laid my six-gun the night before. Next to a John B. and a pair of boots, I reckon the lack of a good six-gun will make a man feel as naked as ever. It's the way of the land.

"What're you trying to do, wake the whole camp, cattle and all?" Wash asked, following the same procedure as I had.

"Hell, somebody's got to!" the cook said with a growl. "Why, you pilgrims would sleep until noon ary I didn't!"

"Some days that ain't a half bad idea," One-Armed Bill said, scratching his head.

Like the rest of the camp that wasn't already up, I splashed some water in my face, did some stretching, and grabbed the cup of coffee the cook was offering along with a plate of what was now nearly a standard fare of beans, a slice or two of bacon, and a biscuit. If you were lucky, there was enough of a syrupy mess on your plate to sop up along with the biscuit to make it look half appetizing. Most of us just ate it before the sun was topping the horizon and tried to imagine it as a better cut of beef we'd had at one time or another in our lives. You know what I mean.

"Cookie, is this the only thing you know how to make for a breakfast meal?" another of the men said in a downtrodden voice.

"Oh, quit your bellyaching, Smitty," Cookie replied in his ever-present growl. "And enjoy the bacon while you can, boy, 'cause once we get this herd a-moving, why, you're gonna be eating beef and beans. *Boiled* beef, at that!"

"You're a joy to be around, Shorty," I said, knowing full well that there ain't a cook alive who didn't have his temperamental side. Hell, just look at the Ferris women and Wash's wife, Sarah Ann, back in Twin Rifles. Nice as you could want a woman to be. But put them in front of a stove with a wooden spoon in their hands and they take on the disposition of a tyrant if ever I've seen one. Yes, sir.

Actually, Shorty Hall, the cook's real name, or at least the name most of the crew knew him by, wasn't a half bad cook. Not at all. Ever since I'd ridden into camp there had been a constant fire going and coffee on the boil if not sitting in an oversize pot next to the fire and ready to pour whenever you'd want some. And considering the fact that there would likely be days when a good cup of hot, strong coffee was all we'd have for a meal, why, I couldn't complain about that at all. There had always been food ready to serve three times a day to the crew and usually in a large enough quantity to fill a man's plate a second time if he so desired. Trouble was that after a day's work on a roundup like this one, a man usually had only enough energy left to wolf down what food he had on his plate, then catch a few winks before his turn at guard came up that night. No one knew for sure, but the camp cook seemed to always be there, always have coffee on the ready, and always have the meals made up on time. How he slept and where, I didn't know. Nor did I care to know. As long as the man could do his job, that was fine with me.

For being as fiery a man as he was, Shorty Hall was not even five and a half feet tall. He might have had close to twenty years on me, which meant he'd been around some, for I considered myself as having been around this land a good deal. His hair was peppered with gray, as was his beard. After seeing the beards on both Hall and Goodnight, I could see how this fashion of wearing full beards had caught on since the end of the war. Old Shorty had a hitch in his git-along, and although he'd never said much about where he'd come from or where he was going, I had a notion he'd be the kind of man who would get along fine with Pa. I say that because Pa had spent the better part of his youth up in what he called the Shinin' Mountains, or the Rockies, free trapping as a mountain man. From the way Shorty spoke every once in a while, I had the idea that he was of that persuasion himself. If you ever come across a man who likes to pepper his language with the word "ary," I'd bet money he was from the mountains known as the Rockies. And Shorty Hall fit that breed of man.

"How about flannel cakes some morning, Cookie? Or is the boss man telling you to feed us this stuff for a reason?" Emmett said, holding his plate up in what can only be described as a look of disgust. Quick as you could blink an eye, Shorty had a large wooden spoon in his hand and was taking a handful of steps toward the ex-sergeant, the spoon raised above his head as though it were some sort of weapon. For a sawed-off runt, Shorty Hall sure could cover a good deal of ground in a short period of time. It took him as many seconds as it did steps to reach Emmett, who looked about as scared as I'd ever seen him.

"Let me tell you something, *flannelmouth,*" Shorty said, waving the threatening spoon at Emmett, "you get me some flour and baking powder and by God I'll make your flapjacks!" It wasn't a threat, the man was talking pure promise from what I could see.

"Whoa, hoss," Emmett said, suddenly pushing a hand out, palm forward, as though to fend off this charging maniac. "Ease off now, pard. I was just talking, you know. Just talking."

"My eye and Betty Martin!" If Shorty Hall didn't

start foaming at the mouth, why, I'll eat my hat. That's how mad he looked. "You was bellyaching, just like all the rest of these yahoos! Bellyaching!"

"How about if I get you that flour and, what, baking powder—is that what you said, Shorty?" I offered, thinking maybe I could save Emmett's life quicklike.

"Well . . ." My words had soothed Shorty's feathers some and made him back off. Flustered him is what I'd done. Someone offering to help him had struck the man as so strange that he couldn't think of anything to say.

"Charlie says he's going into Weatherford for supplies this morning," I added. "I'll tell him to pick you up some of them supplies."

Emmett scowled at me. "And tell him his cook requested 'em under threat of death. Mine!" With that he tossed the plate to the ground, the action being some kind of symbol, I reckon, for it was already empty, already clean as could be. Emmett, I knew, had gone without enough meals to know that the good ones you get are few and far between. I suspicioned he just wasn't saying that Shorty Hall was a better than average cook.

"Done," was all Shorty said as he stuck a paw out to me. I took it, considering the deal struck.

I was about to walk off to find Charlie Goodnight, when Shorty took a grip on my arm and led me off toward his domain of the chuck wagon. He held his finger up to his lip, indicating a request for quiet as he looked around for some intruder who might be listening. Mysterious, real mysterious, I thought.

"What's the matter, Shorty?" I frowned.

"Listen," he whispered to me, "you get Charlie to pick me up some sugar and some dried apples ary you can find any." His face then took on a look of determination as he said, "If these birds don't think I can cook, well, they'll find out."

"Your secret's safe with me, Shorty," I whispered back to the man before leaving to find Charlie.

It wasn't hard to figure out. Flour, baking powder, sugar, and dried apples. Unless I missed my guess, that was pretty much the ingredients of what my own mother had made many a time in my youth.

Shorty Hall was going to dazzle the crew with his version of deep-dish apple pie.

CHAPTER

★ 6 ★

Charlie Goodnight was already saddled to ride when I found him after the breakfast meal. As might be expected, he was damn near everywhere, checking on his men as they continued with the roundup, making sure everything was done just so.

"You still fixing to head for Weatherford today?" I asked him. When he nodded yes, I smiled and related the incident that had just taken place between Shorty and the crew, and the cook's additional request for baking powder and sugar.

"That's Shorty, all right," Charlie said, returning the smile. "That man ain't about to be outdone by no one." I didn't have to tell him what I thought was on Shorty's mind, for I had a notion he already knew what I was only guessing at.

Weatherford was like a lot of towns in Texas back then, big enough to have a couple of hundred inhabitants, but small enough to be unnoticeable next to places such as Austin. Like Fort Belknap, Weatherford lay right on the Brazos River, so it was nothing more than a matter of following the Brazos on its south by east course until we came to the town of Weatherford. The trail we followed was used by a stage line that regularly ran between Fort Belknap and Weatherford, which was just west of Fort Worth.

According to Charlie, Weatherford was the largest town in Parker County and had been selected as the county seat back in April of 1856. A Jefferson Weatherford had been a member of the Texas senate when the county had been organized, so naturally the town had been named for this man. That piece of knowledge alone says a lot for the way politics is played everywhere. The city had been incorporated in 1858 and during the war had formed its first city police force. Tell Pa something like that and he'd likely make a comment about the city becoming civilized.

It took a couple of hours of steady riding, Charlie in his buckboard and me on my horse, but we managed to arrive at the town closing in on midday. Me, I'd have headed for the saloon for a drink, but Charlie Goodnight was all business, so we pulled up in front of the general store first.

"Oh, better add this to the list," Charlie said inside the store, after he'd spoken to the clerk about the items he wanted to order. He then picked up a pencil on the countertop and carefully wrote in sugar and baking powder on the bottom of his list.

"It sure does get hot," I said as we were headed out the door, doffing my John B. and wiping my forearm across my brow.

"No need to prod me, Chance," he replied with a raised eyebrow. "I was going to let you make a stop there now, anyway." He glanced across the street and gave a nod toward the saloon.

But we'd no sooner left the store than we came across a man I gauged to be Charlie Goodnight's size and stature. Apparently, the two knew one another.

"Well, I'll be," Charlie said with a smile and offered the man his hand in greeting. The man smiled back and took Charlie's hand eagerly.

"Can't say as I was looking to meet you here, Charlie," the man said when the pair had finished their howdy-dos.

"Come in for supplies," Charlie said and yanked a thumb over his shoulder at the general store. To me, he said, "Chance Carston, I want you to meet Oliver Loving, one of the best men with a longhorn you'll find in this land." I shook the man's hand and got the same warm smile he had offered Charlie Goodnight. I got the impression he was fairly easygoing.

"Say, Charlie," Loving said, pulling his watch and fob out of his pocket and giving it a gander after the two men had spent a few minutes exchanging pleasantries. "I was about to get something to eat. Why don't you two gents join me?"

What I wanted was a cold beer, but I nodded and said fine when Charlie glanced my way for approval. Hell, the beer was likely only lukewarm anyway. After all, where are you going to find ice in Texas this close to summer?

The eatery we set our git-up ends down at advertised the best plate of meat in town, but after a quick glance around, I decided it was probably the only place in town too. We ordered panfried steaks all around and sat there drinking coffee while the order was being prepared. It's a good thing I wasn't in the inquisitive mood, for the way Charlie was talking I couldn't have gotten a word in edgewise. Apparently, he and this man Loving were good friends, enough so that Charlie Goodnight didn't mind bragging about the man to me.

According to Charlie Goodnight, Oliver Loving could hold his own with any man on any day. Nearly twenty-five years older than Goodnight, Loving had come to Texas a little more than twenty years earlier and had started out farming, freighting, and dealing with livestock. A couple of years before the war he'd partnered up with a man named Durkee and drove a herd of cattle to market in Chicago.

"It's the first time I can recall anyone in Texas driving a herd of cattle to market," Charlie said with a good deal of pride. The waitress brought our plates, but you'd swear Charlie was more interested in talking about his friend than eating the steak, which turned out to be right tasty, by the way.

Oliver Loving had driven a second herd up the Arkansas River to Pueblo and into Denver sometime around 1859. During the war he'd supplied cattle to the Confederacy and come away nearly broke. Wash would like this man, I thought, if for nothing else than that fact.

Charlie was silent for a bit and ate about half of his steak while Oliver Loving and I finished ours. But halfway through the meal, Charlie was back at it again, telling Loving about the herd he was putting together and how he was fixing to get them to Fort Sumner in the New Mexico Territory.

"You're crazy to take the direct route. You'll never

make it through the Indians, Charlie," Loving said when Charlie was through talking.

"Ain't taking the direct route," Charlie quickly said, forking another piece of meat into his mouth. Around the meat, he said, "Gonna run 'em south over the Llano Estacado to Horsehead Crossing and follow the Pecos up to Sumner."

"Then you're still crazy. The heat will do you in that way," Loving said. "There ain't a drop of water on that hundred-mile stretch. You know that, don't you, Charlie?"

"I know. But I've got eighteen of the best men I could find, and I aim to make it. Ain't that right, Chance?" Goodnight said to me.

"That's a fact, Mr. Loving."

Oliver Loving was silent for a while, obviously deeply in thought about something and wanting to say the right thing when he spoke. Finally, he said, "I've got a herd of my own out of town."

"Thought that was your brand I spied when we passed 'em," Charlie said in an offhand manner.

"If you're that determined to go, Charlie, I'll go with you if you'll let me," Loving said. It was nothing more than an offer and was said as such, of that I was sure.

I knew these two men were better acquainted with one another than I was with my own brother when Charlie was eager to reply to the man's proposal. "I'll not only let you," he said in one of his more cheerful tones of voice. "I want you to know it's the most desirable thing of my life." Before he'd gotten all the words out, it was easy to see that Oliver Loving was indeed flattered at Charlie Goodnight's gesture. "Why, I not only need the assistance of your force, I'll need your advice as well."

"Just what is it you want him to do, Charlie?" I asked as the waitress filled my cup with more coffee and took our plates.

"Yes, Charlie, just what is it you'd like me to do?" Oliver Loving said, repeating me.

"Well, I look at it this way. Chance and me are gonna spend most of our time out front of the herd, scouting up water holes and trying to make a trail to follow. And like I told Chance, I don't know of a man better qualified to deal with cattle on a drive like this than you, Oliver. I want you to be the foreman while I'm not in camp. You know, make sure the cattle keep on the trail and the men keep up with their jobs. Now, I know you can do that."

"Only if I can take my herd along," Loving said.

"Agreed and settled," Charlie said and stuck out his hand.

Neither man had to do it, but you might say it was a formality back then, for your word was as good as your bond. A handshake, well, I reckon that sealed the deal.

But I had a notion that with Charlie Goodnight and Oliver Loving, the words "agreed and settled" were all that were needed to know that one could count on the other to carry through his end of the bargain.

CHAPTER

★ 7 ★

It was early June when Goodnight and Loving joined herds about twenty-five miles south of Fort Belknap. There were two thousand head in all. And accompanying them on this journey would be eighteen well-armed men who were just as anxious as the longhorns they'd be driving.

Like some of the other men, I didn't know a damn thing about a cattle drive or what all had to be done once you got the longhorns moving, so Charlie Goodnight called all of us together after breakfast that first morning and explained as best he could what we could look forward to.

"Oliver Loving will be in charge of you men most days while I'm out looking for a new watering hole," he began. "He'll tell you when to start the herd and just how wide it ought to be from one side to the other. The span should be fifty to sixty feet across the herd.

"Under normal conditions, the herd will stop to graze around eleven o'clock in the morning. You'll give 'em about an hour to do so. It's during that time that you'll each have a chance to stop by the mess wagon and eat dinner." To Shorty Hall, he said, "I'll have that spot set up for you as soon as I can each morning."

"Sounds good to me, boss," Shorty said with a nod.

"Once they're through grazing at noon," Charlie continued, "the cattle won't graze again until they reach the next water hole, which should be around sundown. Once they've grazed, you'll bed 'em down, putting 'em in a circle, the cattle being a comfortable distance apart.

"Oliver will show you where you'll be riding each day and what your job entails," he said in conclusion. He was about to turn away when he paused and said, "There is one other thing. Sometime today I want each of you to see Shorty. He's got copies of an agreement each of you needs to sign. It sets forth what each man is expected to do." He turned to Wash and me as he continued to speak. "Like I told the Carston boys when they first got here, I won't have no fighting in my camp or on this drive. Save your energy for working these longhorns. Believe me, you'll need every bit of it. But my main concern is that you all know that there'll be no gunplay on this drive either. If one of you shoots another, you'll be tried by the outfit and hanged if found guilty. If I have anything to say about it, I won't have any of my crew shot on the trail. Dealing with the Comanche, Kiowa, and Apache on this drive is going to be hard enough." He was silent a moment before adding, as though an afterthought or explanation, "A good boss man oughtta make sure his men are safe from not only the Comanche but each other as well."

I reckon that was all that was on his mind, for he simply turned on his heel and headed for his mount, through talking to us for the time being, I reckon.

"All right, boys, let's saddle up and move 'em out," Oliver Loving said, an air of authority about him now. This wasn't the easygoing fellow I'd first met in Weatherford. The command in this man's voice said he was in charge now and there was no question about it.

I don't know about the rest of them, but I had mixed emotions about the whole thing. Oh, I had the feeling of excitement that comes with starting out on any new adventure, that was for sure. In this case, it was sort of like being a modern day Daniel Boone and paving our own version of the Wilderness Trail. Here we were, fixing to blaze a trail that might very well be used by others who would follow us. But there was also that deep-seated pit in my stomach that kept asking me: What if we *don't* make it through? What if Oliver Loving is right and we're all crazy for tempting the gods who send down the heat that only a Texas summer can bring? What if we didn't make it across the dreaded Llano Estacado, and all that was left of us was a pile of bones to be remembered by as fools who tried the impossible? I decided that the best thing to do was put thoughts like that out of my mind, and the only way I knew how to do that was to work so hard I couldn't think about it.

Riding out front with Charlie Goodnight and scouting the area turned out to be a full-time job. As Charlie had said, we rode a good twelve, fifteen, sometimes even twenty miles ahead of the rest of the herd, trying to spot suitable water holes, range and bedding grounds for the herd at the end of the day. For a herd our size, twelve miles a day was average. Fifteen miles a day was pushing it but not unattainable.

For many a mile our course was plain as we followed the trace of the Butterfield Southern Overland Mail route, just as Charlie had planned. Actually, this part of the trail had already been blazed. Men such as Captain R. B. Marcy, the army explorer, Boundary Commissioner John R. Bartlett, and Captain John Pope had been through this area in the 1840s and 1850s. Still, at best this was a tried but uncertain land full of dangers and difficulties.

Oliver Loving did a good job of placing the men. Most caught on to their appointed jobs real quick like, while one or two did the griping for the whole outfit. Most of us stayed busy enough not to have the energy to bellyache about anything.

The work was pretty hard but we made our way west, past Fort Cooper and the gaunt, haunted chimneys of old Fort Phantom Hill. This land is full of legends, one of them being that early western travelers and soldiers had gotten their first glimpses of what are known as mirages on this particular part of the plains area. It was this legend, true or not, that conjured up the Phantom Hill name.

We turned south, still following the trace of the old Southern Mail route, down through Buffalo Gap. Those first few days I still had my mind on the sanity of this trek we were on. It bothered me something fierce, almost as much as missing Sarah Ann bothered my brother, I reckon.

But it was long before we reached the Llano Estacado that I rid myself of those thoughts. And let me tell you, it was one hellacious experience, too!

Sarah Ann was standing in the doorway by the time the stranger pulled up in front of the Carston ranch house. She was dressed in her best Sunday-go-to-meeting clothes. The stranger, a coarse-looking man with dark eyes and hair to match, was of a good size. He reminded her a lot of Chance in that respect, she immediately thought to herself. Still, this one seemed to carry a permanent frown on his forehead, a dangerous look that put her on the defensive right away.

"Can I help you, sir?" she said, as though she were waiting on a table at the Porter Cafe. Her father, Big John Porter, who owned and operated the cafe, had long ago taught her to be polite to people, whether she was waiting tables or not.

The stranger smiled, although Sarah Ann could have sworn it was a leer more than a smile. It was hard telling under what appeared to be close to a week's worth of beard.

"I do believe you can, ma'am. I just come a far piece and I'd lay odds my horse is more tuckered than I am," he said. "The both of us could sure use some water if you've any about."

"There's a trough and a water pump over on the side of the corral," she said, suddenly wanting the man to go, hoping he hadn't picked up the nervousness in her voice. There was just something about him that she didn't like, although she couldn't pin it down, not for the life of her. She only hoped he didn't notice the fear she was abruptly consumed with.

He did.

She stood on the porch while he watered his horse

and grabbed a mouthful of water for himself. For a man who had ridden a long way, he certainly didn't seem too thirsty. For that matter, neither did his horse. This man obviously wasn't after water and the fear grew within her.

"What do you want?" she asked, all too eager to get him out of her life. Perhaps she wouldn't have acted that way if she hadn't seen quite clearly that he was indeed sporting a leer on his face. But in that moment he knew she was afraid of him. "Please go. I don't want any trouble."

"Oh, I won't hurt you, lady . . . I don't think." He said it in a manner that left an awful lot of doubt as to just what it was he would do to Sarah Ann.

"Son, that won't never happen." Sarah Ann looked beside her and let out a grateful sigh of relief. The stranger had momentarily scared her so much that she had forgotten she was having a quiet Sunday dinner with Will Carston, who had taken her to church that morning and spent the better part of the afternoon in her company that day. Up until now it had been an enjoyable time, then the stranger had ridden up. But Will Carston's voice gave her confidence and she didn't feel afraid so much anymore. "You touch so much as a hair on this young lady's head and I'll kill you outright where you stand. And that's that."

"I find that hard to believe, *grandpa,*" the stranger said, his leer suddenly turning lopsided and taking on the form of a sneer.

Before the stranger could get out another smart alecky remark, Will Carston had pulled his Remington .44 from its holster and shot from the hip, sending the stranger's hat flying from his head, a bullet hole in the middle of the crown.

"Believe it, son, believe it," Will said, a certain nastiness creeping into his voice now. Will Carston was a good forty years older than the woman beside him, his iron gray hair a distinct indication that he had been up the creek, over the mountain, down into the cave and back. But he still had a touch of vanity when it came to his age, and he hadn't expected to be addressed as a grandfather until one of his two sons' wives bore him a grandchild. So far that was just Sarah Ann and she didn't look anything close to being with child yet. "Now, just what is it you're a-looking for, flannelmouth?" Will said, all business. Sunday dinner would have to wait. "Aside from trouble, that is?"

The stranger shrugged, poking a finger through the hole in his hat, an act that changed the leer into a hateful frown. "Next to watering my horse, I was looking for a man named Chance Carston. Friend of mine, he is."

"Now, darlin', there's a lesson to be learned here," Will said to Sarah Ann, speaking to his daughter-in-law as though the stranger weren't even there. "What the man said is an out-and-out lie, guaranteed." He said it with a wink and a nod, as though that were all that was needed to certify the truth of his words.

"Calling a man a liar can be awful dangerous, mister," the stranger said, a hint of a growl crawling into his tone. This seemed awful silly to Will, especially since he still had his Remington in his fist and it was still pointed in the general direction of the stranger.

"I reckon there's some truth in that, flannelmouth," Will said. "But it ain't me that's lying, you see. It's you."

"And just how would you know that?" The stranger sounded just a mite shaken now.

"Simple, son, simple. Chance Carston's my son, and I told him more times than he cared to recall not to get mixed up with the likes of hairy-faced plug uglies like you that don't do much more than talk as piss ugly mean as they look." There was fire in the stranger's eyes now, and he doubtless had a whole mouthful to say in reply to Will Carston's comments, but Will wasn't having any of it.

"Now before you go getting tanglefoot of the tongue trying to get all those words out, you save us both some time and get on that sad-looking swayback of yours and ride out of here. My dinner's been getting cold for a good five minutes now and I thoroughly hate cold food. Now git." When the stranger looked at him in disbelief, he added, "Go on, git," as though he were talking to one of the young lads in town he had just pulled out of a peck of trouble.

"One other thing, flannelmouth," Will added as the man mounted up. "Yonder's a town called Twin Rifles," he said, pointing in the direction of the town. Before he spoke next he pulled back the vest of his coat, revealing a deputy U. S. marshal's badge. "It's my town. Don't even bother stopping long enough to pass through."

Will didn't holster his Remington until the man had ridden nearly out of sight, he was that distrustful of him. But when he did holster the gun, he found Sarah Ann in his arms, holding on to him for dear life.

"Oh, Papa Will, he scared me so," she said in a muffled voice filled with sobs.

"There, there, child," Will said, patting the girl on

the back for reassurance. "It's all right now. He's gone. He ain't gonna bother us again."

But as they went into the ranch house and Sarah Ann warmed up his meal, Will Carston found himself doubting his own words.

Silently, Sarah Ann had that same doubt.

CHAPTER
★ 8 ★

The fellow's name was Holyoake and for the most part he was a likable cuss. Not only that, he was good with a rope and professed to know a good deal about these longhorns, having worked with the likes of Loving before this drive. Like I said, it was those first couple of days out of Belknap and we were lucky as could be. I say that because Charlie Goodnight had made certain we all knew that we could expect the herd to stampede any old time, day or night. I reckon he'd parlayed with Oliver Loving and the two had come to the conclusion that it would take a few days to get this herd of longhorns settled in and used to having eighteen men around them and pushing them in a direction they likely didn't want to go in the first place.

"They can be spooky, these critters, so you keep a sharp eye out, especially when you're pulling your night watch," Charlie said with deep concern.

It was the third night out that I pulled night guard with Holyoake. When we reached the bedding ground most of the cattle were already down and looking fairly comfortable. I took that as a good sign and, being in open country, could only hope that things would look good for the night. Or at least my watch.

It had been hotter than the devil all day, so the slight breeze that came up that night felt right kind to me. The trouble was that out west I could swear I saw some real nasty looking clouds just hanging around that new moon that had breached the skyline. It was a storm all right, but it was so far off you could barely hear it making so much as a rumble. But like the oldest man in town, you can bet she's walking her way toward me, sure as could be. Mind you, the cattle were all laying there, nice and quiet, but that didn't stop me from getting a worrisome feeling in the pit of my gut.

"They're awful goddamn quiet," I said to Holyoake, the first time I passed him that night.

"Quieter than a nuns' convention, if you ask me," he said.

"Got you bothered too, does it?"

"Some," he nodded. When he was silent once more, I decided it was time to find out if any of these strange gut feelings I was having held any water and asked him for his own thoughts on what exactly was bothering him. "Well, Chance, it's like this. I don't mind cattle laying still, you understand. But I want to hear some kind of natural noises that goes into a herd this size. I want to hear these critters blowing off, or the creaking sound their joints make, something that shows they're easing themselves into their beds. You get my drift?"

I nodded.

"Well, you take a listen, hoss, and if you hear anything about now, I'll eat your saddle, rope and all," he added with only half a smile.

I hadn't noticed anything until then, but when I did listen up, why, it was as quiet as a graveyard. Hell, if it hadn't been for the lightning in the distance every once in a while, why, I likely couldn't have told you there were just over two thousand longhorns bedded down out there in front of me, it was that quiet. Suddenly I felt a chill down my spine, a chill that sent a good deal of fear through me at the same time. Eerie wasn't the word to use to describe it.

It was getting darker every minute and if Holyoake hadn't had his yellow slicker on, I wouldn't have been able to see him beside me. Why, it was so dark you couldn't find your nose with both hands!

"I wonder what time it is," I said to Holyoake. Most times I could use the Big Dipper to tell the time on my turn at a night watch, but I couldn't see the stars, much less the sky they filled.

"Let me find my timepiece and I'll let you know," he said. He hunted around in his pockets a moment, but instead of his fob and pocket watch came up with the fixings and rolled himself a cigarette. At first I was bewildered at the man's actions, but when he got the makings going, he took a long pull on the cigarette and quickly used the light of the tip to read the pocket watch which suddenly materialized in his other hand. "Half past nine," he said, squinting before he was able to make out the watch face.

"Another half hour," I said, breathing a sigh of

relief. "You gonna wake up the next guards or leave it to Emmett and Cimarron?" Sometimes the horse wranglers would take a hand in waking the next guards and have them and their mounts ready for posting when you rode back into camp.

"I don't know," Holyoake said, the light of his cigarette showing me a look of doubt about him now. For as easygoing as he impressed me as being, this didn't seem like the man at all. "I got a notion there's only gonna be one guard on this herd tonight," he said, stripping his cigarette as he spoke. A flash of lightning broke through the clouds in the distance, but it was enough for me to see the intense look on his face as he seemed to stare straight into my eyes and said, "And I got an idea it's just you and me, brother." His words shook me, to be sure, and I honest to God didn't know what to say to the man. Then, as though the conversation were suddenly over, Holyoake added, "Well, I reckon I'll move along. See you."

It was the strangest goddamn thing I'd ever had said to me! Not since I'd had to put up with some of the men who'd been in the thick of fighting for quite a while and seemed to have a permanent madness about them, not since then had I dealt with the likes of this type man. And I didn't like it, not one damn bit!

The lightning continued its silent march toward us. Not that it was making all sorts of noise, you understand, but just seeing it coming my way gave me the certain knowledge that something bad was about to happen before the night was over. Hearing Holyoake spout off the way he had, well, that didn't help matters none, I can guarantee you.

It didn't seem to do any good to ride, for every few seconds the lightning would show me the entire herd out in front of me and I could easily see the lot of them, all bedded down nice and quiet like, just like they were supposed to be. Seeing that lightning was an eerie experience, for one second it could be as light as broad daylight and the next it's as dark as the dungeons of hell itself. Little fireballs began dancing between my horse's ears, adding to the bizarre aura of the night. You spit into the night and the sound is the same as you'd hear on a sulfur match being struck.

Across the way I could see Holyoake, who had positioned himself on the far side of the herd. Above the sputter of the distant thunder and lightning, I could hear him sing his song, doing his best to keep the herd peaceful and calm. Some men will sing whatever songs they know to keep the cattle in place, while others have got their own little lullabies they've made up that accomplish the same thing. Holyoake's song was an old church hymn I'd heard back in my youth, which may be the only reason I recognized it, me not being much of a churchgoer anymore.

Then I saw a steer situated on the edge of the herd, and I knew in a moment it was a bad sign. Oh, he was sitting there peaceful as could be, all right. But he was taking in long draws of air, as though he was nosing for something, smelling trouble his own self. If he's looking for trouble he ain't going to need much of an excuse. Me, I took a sniff of the air too, just to see what it was he thought he could smell. After a lungful or two of air, I thought I smelled something foreign in the air too, something I hadn't smelled since we'd been on the trail.

Now, hoss, damn near every steer will hold his breath for a few seconds and then blow off when he's bedding down. I may not know a hell of a lot about these longhorns and cattle in general, but I'd been paying attention to Goodnight and Loving and their conversations about these critters and thought I'd picked up a thing or two. It's when that damn fool curls up his nose and makes those long draws of air that it's a sign he's hunting up something. All he's got to do is smell something that crosses his wind that he don't like and it's sure to fetch trouble to start with. No doubt about it.

I started riding around, soon tiring of sitting there doing nothing. It was giving me the willies, sitting there and waiting for something to happen. Me, I've got to be doing something, so I started riding my way around the herd again.

Pitch black doesn't come anywhere near to close to describing the light there wasn't to see with right then. It was almost as though the fires of hell had gone out and all that was left was the dark of night, and I don't mind telling you it was a scary kind of darkness. Or maybe that was because in a moment I could hear as well as feel many of the cattle in the herd start to rise.

Mind you, now, I'm no singer, no singer at all. Why, they wouldn't even let me sing in the tub those few times I got a chance to clean myself off during the war, my voice was that bad. But at that particular moment, friend, I really didn't care. I knew that riding was useless, so I simply reached down in my gut and pulled out the sounds and what I thought were the words to one of those slow moving hymns they used to make us sing every Sunday. If I couldn't soothe these critters with my voice, maybe I could obfuscate them. Hell, it was worth a try.

I don't know if it was my voice or just one of Mother Nature's cruel tricks, but abruptly the lightning stopped, as did the breeze. The silence was deadly and the heat was worse than it had been when the sun was out.

But it didn't seem to bother Holyoake, for his voice didn't falter one bit but kept on with more of his lullabies. I was trying to figure out how he did it, when I swear I heard a sort of whisper in the grass around me as the breeze quickly picked up again. Then it seemed as though the ground began to shake and every one of those longhorns was running.

My horse too. He took off, scared as the cattle, and busted a hole in the darkness when he threw both front feet in a badger hole and went down on his knees and plowed his nose into the dirt. But he was a good night horse and hard to keep down, and the minute he had his feet under him, why, he was up on all fours and running like a frightened wolf. I had my head turned over my shoulder, trying to see what direction the herd was going in, when another flash of lightning burst through the darkness, leaving a big hole in the sky. It was the kind that will make a believer out of any man, thunder, lightning and all, if you know what I mean. It was then my horse whirled and stopped in his tracks, almost as though he were as scared of what was taking place as me. I swear I could feel his heart pumping away wildlike against my knee, although I'd also swear that it couldn't have been going any faster than my own heart. I reckon we were both plenty jittery just then.

When a flash lit up the sky, I could see most of the herd running to my left. The next thing I knew, big drops of rain were falling and the storm that had accompanied the thunder and lightning was upon us. In fact, when a second flash showed itself in the sky, I could see Holyoake not far away from me.

"Ain't been through nothing like this since the war, amigo," I yelled to him.

"Yeah," he yelled back in agreement. "I wonder

who kicked the lid off this teapot?" If he meant is all hell breaking loose, I sure couldn't tell him.

There was no clicking of their horns, so I knew the cattle were running straight. I also knew there was no way I could control them in this kind of weather, so I simply stayed wide of the herd and played the whole thing by ear. I didn't have to wait long. They only ran for a short ways before beginning to crowd together again. Soon they were milling about, their heads jammed together as their horns locked with one another.

Then something strange happened. There was another occurrence of a bolt of lightning, followed by the sight of Holyoake mixed in with the milling cattle. In that one brief second I thought I heard two or three shots going off from a six-gun. Could it be Holyoake trying to shoot his way out of that bunch of mad and confused longhorns? Maybe so. Maybe not. All I knew at the moment was that it was hard enough for me to keep astride of my own saddle. Like a Comanche raiding party, the storm had stopped as quickly as it had started. Oh, there were still occasional bolts of lightning in the sky, but I couldn't see Holyoake anymore, couldn't see him anywhere, not even his horse.

The herd seemed to settle down after that, the storm clearing for the night. My relief showed up and I turned in my mount, both of us pretty much tired out by the evening's events.

"You seen Holyoake yet?" I asked Emmett, who was as wide awake as everyone else in camp since the stampede had begun.

"Nope, can't say as I have," he replied. "Wasn't he out there with you?"

"Yeah." An unsettling feeling hung in my belly

about then as the events of the night and Holyoake's comments crossed my mind in what could only have been a fleeting second. "But I've got a notion he ain't coming back."

"I see." My words must have been contagious, for I got the specific premonition that Emmett knew what I was talking about. Whether he did or not, he didn't say any more, not that night, anyway.

The only reason I slept was because I was so damned tired. I thought I'd lay there all night—or what was left of it—and ponder on what had happened to Holyoake. But I didn't. I fell instantly asleep, although I have to admit it was a fitful sleep at best.

Stampede or no stampede, Shorty had a meal ready for us at first light, and I was right there to get my fill. But I ate in silence and saw Emmett about to mount his horse.

"He never showed up, Chance," he said even before I could ask him if Holyoake had come in during the night. I knew then I had to search the area of the stampede, had to find Holyoake. You learn to stick by the men you work with in this land, and Holyoake was no different than any of the rest of the crew. I just didn't know him as well as I did Emmett.

I followed the back trail of the stampede for a good three hundred yards, being careful to look about for what I might find—for what I was truly afraid I'd find. My heart jumped to my throat when I finally saw him.

If it hadn't been for that yellow slicker he wore, I likely wouldn't have seen Holyoake. As it was, there was little enough of him left and it had been trampled into the ground from the looks of it. The man I'd known as Holyoake was missing his six-gun, so perhaps it was indeed him I'd heard firing what sounded like a pistol the night before. Damn near all of his body had been crushed, with the exception of his chest, shoulders, and head. Blood and surrounding mud had been mixed up pretty well by the longhorns as they crushed the man's body.

"Hell," I heard a voice behind me say, and turned to see Charlie Goodnight and One-Armed Bill Wilson on horseback. "Get some shovels, Bill. We'll bury the boy where he lays."

And that's exactly what we did.

"Any idea what caused that stampede last night, Charlie?" I asked as we dug Holyoake's grave. I related to him what I'd seen before all hell broke loose and asked if it might not have been the thunder and lightning. But Charlie must have caught on to what I said about the smelling the longhorns had been doing just before the stampede.

"Sounds to me like some of those wolves I seen in the area yesterday," he said. "Longhorns get a whiff of something foreign like that and I've no doubt it'll set 'em to running."

So it was wolves that had put a good man in the ground only three days out of Fort Belknap. You can bet your bottom dollar I took a real dislike to the wolf species from that day forward.

CHAPTER

★ 9 ★

"Wash, why don't you go with Chance today and help him scout out the next water hole," Charlie Goodnight said the next morning as we ate.

My brother shrugged. "Whatever you say, boss." He was about to let it go at that when something must have hit him and it wasn't long before he spit it out. "Say, does this have anything to do with how I'm doing my job?" he asked Charlie as the man began to walk away.

"Not at all, Wash." Wash had been helping out Emmett and Cimarron with the remuda ever since the drive had begun. Truth to tell, I hadn't seen much of him, being out most of the day with Charlie as we hunted up water holes, grazing and bedding grounds. We'd all worked pretty hard at the start, not having much time for palavering at the end of the day. Some of that would change, I was sure, once the herd settled down and everyone knew their job better. "I'm gonna stay behind and give Emmett a hand today with the mounts. There's a few other things I want him to know about how these mustangs of ours need to be handled. Nothing personal at all."

"Suits me," Wash said, and Charlie was gone.

It wasn't long before we were saddled and on our way. We were still in Indian territory, specifically Comanche, and I was expecting to see a war party appear out of nowhere any minute now. But if you want to know the truth, I'd rather have Wash with me than anyone else if and when that happened. We'd both been off to war and survived, we'd fought the Comanche back to back, not to mention Comancheros, and I knew him to be as good at fighting Indians as I thought I was. So I knew he was as much on the lookout for them when we left as I was.

"Too bad about Holyoake," Wash said not far out of camp. I'd be a liar if I didn't admit that Holyoake's death still weighed on my mind some.

"Part of living out here, I reckon," I replied, not wanting him to think I was greatly disturbed by the matter. "You play your cards and take your chances." And that was that, as far as Holyoake was concerned.

A little farther out I asked Wash how he was dealing with missing Sarah Ann.

"A mite better, I reckon, but I still miss her."

"Good. I'd hate to have Charlie Goodnight on my back about anything," I said, which was true. Like the rest of the crew, I was learning that Charlie could be a hard taskmaster.

The land we were traveling was pretty much flat, although it did have what seemed like a hilly portion or two every once in a while. We took our time that morning, riding maybe a couple of hours and taking it easy before we came to an area that looked suitable for the noon grazing.

"Want me to ride on back and let Shorty know where to set up noon camp?" Wash asked.

I was about to tell my brother to do exactly that when I caught something out of the corner of my eye. But before I could do anything they were there.

A Comanche war party.

There might have been a dozen of them if I'd taken the time to count them proper. All I knew was they were armed and ready for a fight and as much as I was wanting to pull my Colt and lay into them, my survival instinct was telling me I'd better not. Not that I'm against a good fight, you understand. It's just that sometimes it's better to pull your freight than pull your gun. Trouble was, I had a notion these fellows might just backshoot us if we tried making a run for it. A casual glance at Wash told me he was mulling over the same thoughts.

"Howdy, gents," Wash said, tipping his hat and doing his damnedest to smile in the process. Leave it to my brother to try to make light of the situation.

The big one leading this bunch held up his hand, palm forward, and said the same thing, I reckon, in his own language. So far no one had made any motions to throw down on us, which was always a good sign. Who knew, maybe they were a friendly bunch. Not that I was counting on it, you understand, but who knew?

I took off my hat and wiped the sweat off my brow, looking skyward for a moment. "Looks like it's gonna be a hot one," I said in as calm a voice as I could muster.

This time the answer came in what you might call

the language of the plains when it came to communicating with an Indian, that language being sign language. Pa had taught Wash and me this basic form of discussion in our youth and it hadn't changed much.

All the time this so-called conversation was taking place, I found myself taking in the features of the big one, the leader of this bunch. It was then I noticed something strange about him that didn't fit the rest of the warriors he was with.

He had blue eyes!

Now hoss, you just don't find that in an Indian, I don't care what tribe he's from. Nearly every Indian I'd ever seen had black hair and eyes to match. You wouldn't find anything else on one of them . . . unless he was a half-breed. At first I squinted at this man, then saw he'd noticed my actions and was doing the same to me. I was running it all through my mind when it came to me. If he was a Comanche, and he was a Comanche, this could only be one man.

"Quanah? Quanah Parker?" I said, certain I'd tagged him right.

"You know?" he asked in broken English.

"With those eyes, it had to be you," I said, feeling a little more at ease.

Quanah Parker was the son of a captured white woman by the name of Cynthia Ann Parker, who had been kidnapped by the Comanche back in 1836. That she was still alive or had lived long enough to foster a child was likely a miracle in itself. But I'd heard of Quanah, who had been raised as a full-blooded Comanche even though he was a half-breed of sorts. He was part of the Kwahadi band of the Comanche and had made himself a reputation since the War Between the States had taken place. He wasn't a chief or anything that I knew of, but some folks just stand out in whatever they do, and Quanah Parker was one such person.

He got curious. He wanted to know if we were Texans.

"Think he's getting moral about who he kills?" Wash asked.

"Beats the hell outta me." To Quanah Parker I used sign language and explained that we were simply brothers who had come west after fighting a war. Americanos is the word I used to describe us. You have to realize that the Comanche purely hates the Texan. It's been that way ever since the Council House Fight back in '41, but that's a whole 'nother canyon, as Pa likes to say. Being an Americano, well, that's a slightly different proposition with the Comanche. Hell, you might even come away with your scalp if they found out you were simply an Americano. And that was what my intent was, coming away from this meeting with my hair still in one piece, namely on top of my head.

"I'm scouting for a herd of cattle back yonder," I added, tossing a thumb over my shoulder. "Just passing through. Looking for some water and grazing land." I was trying to keep it as simple as possible.

Quanah Parker nodded, understanding me so far, I reckon.

I noticed he was carrying both a rifle and a bow and arrows. Then, for whatever reason I couldn't really tell you, Holyoake and the way he died crossed my mind. Charlie Goodnight had said it was likely wolves he had spotted earlier that day, wolves that were following the herd. What if those wolves decided to investigate our camp again tonight? What if they started another stampede by their presence? What if another man was trod over the way Holyoake had been? What if it was *me* this time? It was time to do some horse trading.

"Does a man as brave as you need two weapons to fend off his foes?" I asked Quanah. Granted my comment might come close to starting a fight between the two of us, but like I said, it was time to do some horse trading.

"Sometimes my hands are the only weapons I need," was his reply. I had no doubt of the truth of those words.

"I need to trade you for your bow and arrow," I said flat out. This was about as tactful as I was going to get.

He cocked his head sideways for a moment, giving me a strange look, as though I had a lot of guts to make such an offer. Hell, I wasn't even a Comanchero.

"What do you have to trade?"

"A possession equal to your bow and arrow, if not more precious."

"What have you got in mind?" Wash asked with a frown, just as befuddled as Quanah Parker, I thought.

"Go back and tell Shorty where our noon camp will be," I said. "Then get Emmett to cut that paint out of the remuda for you and bring it here." I thought he saw what I was getting at. To Quanah I said, "My brother goes to get the prize."

Quanah Parker muttered some Comanche to his warriors, which I took to mean that they wouldn't shoot at Wash when he left. It did.

Wash must have rode hell-for-leather, for he was back in an hour with the paint mustang we'd picked up along the way. Like I said, paints ain't much good for nothing but riding into town, and these Indians always did like colorful mounts.

"In trade for your bow and arrow," I said, gently handing the roped horse to Quanah.

It was a trade all right, and Quanah Parker was getting the better part of it and he knew it. He slid off his own mount and inspected the paint. He patted it alongside the neck, then held its mouth open to inspect the horse's teeth. Then he breathed on the horse, which I'd seen done before by some old-timers who swore that letting the horse get a whiff of who you were was as good an introduction as you could give the mount.

"Why do you want my bow and arrow?" Quanah wanted to know next.

I set to explaining to the man about the stampede and Holyoake and how he'd died and how my boss claimed it likely was a pack of wolves that the longhorns had gotten scent of that made them run scared. I tried to explain that I planned on hunting the wolves down and killing them, but that to fire a weapon around the herd would only start another stampede and I didn't want that. What I needed was a silent weapon like his bow and arrow.

He seemed to understand. One more look at the horse and he stripped himself of his bow and arrow. He could always make himself another one of those weapons.

"One other thing," I said when the transaction was completed.

"What?"

"I'd appreciate it if you'd tell others of your tribe that the men on this cattle drive of mine are all Americanos and not Texans," I said. "We come in peace and are only passing through. We mean no one any harm."

"It is done."

That was fine with me. Hell, you couldn't ask for better than that. Safe passage through the territory, or at least as far as these Comanche roamed.

"Now, what in the world was that?" Shorty asked not ten minutes later as he pulled his chuck wagon to a halt. Quanah Parker and his warriors had just left.

"Just passing the time of day with the local Kwahadi, Cookie," I said with a leer. Shorty gave me a disbelieving look. "Say," I continued, "you carry some kind of poison, don't you?"

"Why sure," he said, then in a secretive aside, adding, "But it's my own personal home brew, you understand."

I gave him a hard look. I wasn't in the mood for some runt with a Napoleon line of thought passing off a sense of humor on me. Not now.

"Say, you're serious, ain't you?" he said, an astonished look about him. When I nodded in silence, he said, "Strychnine." It was what I wanted to hear.

"Why don't you dig it out. I'm gonna need it for a mite."

He didn't make any bones about my request. When he had it out, I gave the arrows in my quiver a quick dosage of the poison and gave the poison back to Shorty.

We found the water for that day and our evening camp about seven miles further on. No war party bothered us.

And by the time the sun set on our camp, there were three dead wolves who would never bother us again either.

CHAPTER

★ 10 ★

For as long as the days were and as hard as we all worked, it surprised me that we got along as well as we did. I reckon we'd all taken to heart the seriousness of the matter of getting these longhorns to market. Or maybe it was the certain knowledge throughout the crew that Charlie Goodnight would indeed turn a man loose for not doing his job, no matter how badly he might need him. I reckon I wasn't the only one who was learning a lot about Charlie Goodnight and his ways.

Then there was Temple, whose powers of learning had been in doubt ever since I'd laid eyes on him. He'd arrived in camp just after Wash, Emmett, and me and had been signed on as one of the crew. He was a belligerent, flannel-mouthed bully who I gauged couldn't see past the end of the day and wanted nothing more complicated than his own way. He sure could bellyache a lot, not to mention make trouble. But I'm getting ahead of myself.

The Concho River runs like a crooked three-pronged pitchfork that points west at varying degrees. We'd crossed the North Concho not long after leaving Fort Belknap that first week on the trail. The South Concho, which is the bottom prong of this pitchfork, runs south by west until it forms what is called the Concho River proper, if you like those fancy names. It's down around a trading post they called San Angelo. There was talk they might build a fort in that vicinity, a prospect Pa had found interesting of late, what with his constant brushes with the Comanche down around Twin Rifles. (I'd found myself wondering if Quanah Parker and his little band had ever raided around that area.) *Concha* is the Spanish word for shell, likely given the rivers that moniker because of the numerous mussel shells found along much of the riverbed areas. I even heard there was a fellow by the name of Diego del Castillo back in the mid 1600s who supposedly came across these tributaries. I reckon he was one of those Spanish blue bloods or adventurers who'd been sent by the queen to find riches or the fountain of youth in the new world. I never could keep track of which was which; just a bunch of money grabbers as far as I'm concerned.

But it was the Middle Concho River, the tributary forming the middle prong that had our attention now, for we had pulled up to it with instructions to let the cattle swim and drink as much as the damn critters could hold.

"How come?" I asked Charlie when he gave the order.

He took me off to the side of the herd and pointed across the river to the west. "You see that flat land out there, Chance?" he said, squinting as he spoke.

I gazed at the vast area he was covering with the wide sweep of his arm, an area that seemed to go from as far north to as far south as I could see. If there were dips in that chunk of land, either I didn't see them or they were well hidden from me. If there were mountains in the distance, they were one hell of a ways off, of that I was sure. What I could see was just what Charlie had called it. Flat land.

"Yeah."

"Well, that's the *Llano Estacado.*"

The words came out with a dangerous, cold chill to them that transferred itself to my very being. The Staked Plains. I'd been so busy with the cattle and water holes and bedding ground that I'd clean forgotten that one of these days we'd come to this area. And that when we did, I'd dread the certain knowledge that we'd have to cross it. It was that feeling that shuddered through me now.

"Don't blame you," Charlie said, apparently seeing what the sound of the words did to me. "You still up to it?"

"I reckon," I said. "I never really liked killing people, but I never cut and run from my duties as a ranger or a soldier," I added, just so he'd know. "Besides, Pa said duty was duty and that was that."

"Sounds like you learned a lot from him."

I smiled, trying to cover some of the fear I was feeling. "I try to let him think so."

Charlie was about to turn to go when he stopped, looking back at me as he added, "What about your brother? You think Wash is up to this? Him being as worried as he is about that woman of his and all?"

I was about to tell Charlie Goodnight that I'd stand by my brother and his ability to function in damn near any situation more than I would just about anyone but Pa. The trouble was I never got to say it.

"Yeah, what about that lazy ass brother of yours, Carston?" Mind you now, I hate to be interrupted, so hearing the voice put me on the defensive right off. I reckon it was seeing that it belonged to Temple when I looked over my shoulder that made me that much the madder.

"That ain't a smart thing to say, Temple," I said, a frown of dissatisfaction now covering my face.

"The hell you say!" the man challenged in a defiant manner.

"Back off, Temple," Charlie Goodnight said, taking a hand in this conversation. But why not, he was the boss. "Chance is right, you got no call to talk like that."

"I'll say what the hell I want, when I want, mister," Temple growled. Apparently, he wasn't in the mood to take any guff from anyone.

Charlie's voice took on a growl now too. "Let's get something straight, *mister,*" he said, his eyebrows coming together in a mean look. "You want to call me mister, you make damn sure you tack Goodnight on after it. You understand me?"

"Like I said—" Temple started to say in his blustery way.

"I don't give a damn what you think or say," Charlie burst out, "I asked you if you understand! Now, do you or don't you?" By the time he was through speaking—or maybe yelling was a better term to use—his arm had shot out at Temple and I do believe that if he was any closer he would have poked the man in the chest hard enough to push him off his mount. "Come on, what'll it be?" he added when Temple was silent for a few moments. It wasn't that the man couldn't find any words to answer with, although I'd have accepted that as an adequate reason for him not saying anything, so much as the fact that Charlie Goodnight had scared the living bejesus out of the big bully. Hell, even I could see that.

"I understand," Temple finally said in a tone of voice that was considerably fainter than his usual stormy way of speaking.

"Good. Now that that's settled, get your sorry ass back to that herd," Charlie added. "And Temple?"

"Yeah?"

"You start any more trouble on this drive and it'll be your last. Make sure you understand that, too," Charlie said, the hardness in his voice unchanged.

Temple didn't say anything else, but reined his horse to the right and headed back to the herd.

"Wash'll do fine," I said, when Temple was gone. "Emmett tells me he's trying to concentrate on working that remuda and doing better and better each day."

"That's all I wanted to know." Then Charlie Goodnight was gone too, leaving me to sit in my saddle alone and take in the wide expanse of land before me.

The whole area, this Llano Estacado, just sort of appeared out of nowhere. It was definitely something God had forgotten to cultivate when making this earth, I'll give Him that. According to Charlie, there were three big draws that stuck out like big fingers if you looked at them right. Centralia Draw, the one we were facing now, was the one we'd be taking on our trek across this hard desert land.

"Shorty, I want you to make sure both of your water barrels are full, as well as those extra canteens, once we get to moving these longhorns out again," Charlie said at the evening meal that night. "Same thing goes with you men. Pass it on that I want every man to make sure his canteen is full when we move out."

I got the impression that no one would have to be told twice to do that. Most of these men, had they not fought in the War Between the States—or a war of one sort or another—had been around long enough to have gone without water for at least a short period of time. And even a short length of time will make you more observant when setting out across a land as dry as the one to our west.

We spent three days preparing for the move across that desert area. Don't think we did nothing more than sit around and play old maid either! We gathered firewood when we weren't keeping an eye on the herd. I reckon Shorty knew that most men on the drive would complain about his cooking, but they seemed to put that aside for the moment as they helped him ready his gear, all of which included gathering up as much extra firewood or deadwood as possible and filling every available container with extra water that last day.

It was the afternoon of the third day that Charlie Goodnight pointed the herd west and we moved out, heading for the setting sun. We trailed the herd late into the night, then camped for the night and moved on at first light the next day.

Most times on the drive these cattle had watered themselves everyday. As little as I'd been around the herd, I'd picked up that one small piece of information. I reckon they reminded me of humans a lot, for I was used to getting a fair amount of water on a daily basis too. But I'll tell you, hoss, at the end of that first day both the men and the cattle were so damned dry from thirst that we couldn't believe it. The day had been long and hot; in fact, it seemed that the further we got into the month of June and the farther west we headed, why, the hotter it got. At the end of our first day trailing across the Llano Estacado, the cattle were simply too thirsty and restless to bed down. I swear that they spent all night milling about and wandering all over the place, but never settling down like they should have. Hell, it took most of the eighteen of us out there all night to keep them from wandering off from the area we'd stopped at.

Charlie Goodnight was none too happy come daybreak.

"Mr. Loving, this will never do," he said to his partner over coffee and hardtack.

"Agreed," said Loving, who was eating the same thing as Charlie. Hell, we were all eating and drinking the same thing. Coffee and hardtack. Of course, by then most of us were eating it either because we knew our bodies needed the energy to keep on moving—in which case we were a lot better off than the horses and cattle, for there wasn't a blade of grass in sight anywhere—or we did it out of pure force of habit. After all, eating and a few winks of sleep seemed to be the only reason to come into camp anymore.

"Those cattle walked enough last night to have got to the Pecos. This camping won't work; we've got to let 'em travel."

"I reckon you're right, Charlie," the older man said, taking another sip of coffee. "It's your herd. You take charge of 'em and see what you can do."

And that was that. The day turned out to be a repeat of the previous day—we worked just as hard as the cattle, watching them grow wearier by each mile and knowing that the only things keeping them going were eighteen cowhands who were likely just as sleepy and tired as they were.

The sun beat down from a sky that can only be described as merciless and we sucked our canteens dry by sundown. It wasn't until the end of that day that we found out that the water barrels had been all but emptied as well. It was enough to make a man want to lay down and die, right then and there.

It may sound like I'm passing on the feelings of most of those eighteen men, but I'm telling you the truth, hoss. I'll admit that I'd had it pretty good so far, doing nothing but riding out a ways and searching for the day's water and bedding grounds and grazing. But what with coming on this Llano Estacado, why, my job sort of disappeared. And there ain't no use in riding a hundred miles ahead just to see if the Pecos River is still at Horsehead Crossing. The Pecos wasn't a river to shift so much, not like the Rio Grande would on a yearly basis. We all knew it would be there. It was just that we had to get across a hundred miles of nothing but slate type dust and rock.

What I wound up doing was riding along with the herd, just like the rest of the men, except for Wash, Emmett, and Cimarron, who handled the remuda. But even they suffered from the bitter white dust that rose in cloudlike formations and all but choked us as we moved the cattle on. Hell, by the end of the first hour out that day, we all looked like bank robbers and highwaymen at best. My eyes were already bleary. By noon my lips cracked like so much dried busted rock. And my throat, well, it was worse than parched. It could have been burning with the fires of hell, as much water as it hadn't had and as much alkali that had stuck in it throughout the day's work. So you see, hoss,

I'm not exaggerating one bit about how we felt, for I've no doubt it was exactly how I was feeling.

The pointers had done a fair job of holding back the leaders. At the rear, the drag hands were fighting the weak stuff, moving 'em forward with hoarse shouts and cussing that could somehow be heard above the bawling and moaning of thirsty cattle.

It was late in the afternoon that I noticed the ribs of many of the longhorns standing out like so many bars on a jail cell. The flanks of these beasts, for that was indeed what they acted like by now, were as drawn and gaunt as I ever thought I'd see an animal, any animal, get. Their tongues would loll out of their heads, often sweeping low enough to seem to be taking on the alkali dust they trod over. If ever there was a bunch of animals that had death in their eyes, it was these two thousand longhorns. Every last damn one of them. On more than one occasion I saw one of them get wild-eyed, turn and make an attempt to fight. After the second one dropped dead, I didn't even bother trying to move them back into the herd. Hell, when they got that wild-eyed look, why, hoss, it was all over. The damn fools were dead on their feet. They just didn't know it!

I reckon what really surprised me was that none of the men fell over as dead as any of those longhorns. Mind you, what these men were doing to keep the herd moving was putting one hell of a strain on them, although no one said much about it. Why, as taut and keen as the nerves grew on most of us, you'd figure most of these men would be ready to jump down one another's throats. I'd been in instances like this during the war when best friends had fallen out with one another, ready to fight and kill to the death over the smallest thing. And not a goddamn person within reach of them would interrupt, for he knew he might be as dead as the intended victim likely would wind up. It was pure madness, I tell you! But somehow we held it together, the whole outfit. Don't ask me how, but we did.

As for Charlie Goodnight, I doubt that he got three winks of sleep, much less three nights that whole time we were crossing the Llano Estacado. Every time I turned around he was in the saddle, sitting atop that big black of his and directing movement here and movement there. It was almost as though he were made to command, and command he did.

I do believe old Oliver Loving had more patience than all of us. Or maybe it was more cow experience, if you believed Charlie Goodnight. The man was constantly working the drag, helping keep as many of the poor critters that wanted to give up the ghost from doing just that. Between you and me, he was a better man than I was; at least at this cow driving trade.

If there was anyone who came close to saving the day, I reckon it was Shorty Hall. The intolerable heat didn't seem to faze the man at all. But then he was used to working over one hell of a hot dutch oven, so maybe he'd adjusted to it better than the rest of us. All I know is I'm glad he did. As constantly as we were on the move, we never really stopped anywhere. But Shorty managed to keep food ready for us to grab a hold of in the saddle as we rode by him. How he did it, I don't know. Was it possible to start a fire inside that chuck wagon of his? Hell, I didn't know, nor did I care. All I knew was he had grub to hand out when I was needing it. And when the water barrels and our canteens were bone dry the end of that second day, low and behold but there was Shorty, handing out a cup of hot coffee for damn near every man in camp! *Hot* coffee, mind you, but liquid just the same. I do believe we were too damned busy drinking the hot stuff to think about asking where the water for the coffee had come from. All but me. I've always been a mite on the nosy side.

"Say, Shorty—" I started to say as I handing him my cup, now as bone dry as I figured my throat had been all day.

"Don't even ask," was all he'd say as he snatched my cup and tossed it in the back of the wagon. "Don't even ask."

"Look at it this way, hoss," Emmett, who I hadn't seen in some time, said. "If them churchgoers ever git to doubting miracles, you just tell 'em they'd better believe 'cause you've seen one with your own eyes."

Then he was gone, back to tending the remuda, I reckon.

Even so, his words made me laugh, and I knew that I'd make it across this damned desert. I just knew it.

Or maybe it was that hot cup of coffee at the end of one of the hottest days I thought I'd ever spend on this earth.

"Gimme a cup of whatever Carston's got, Cookie," Temple said, riding up to the chuck wagon when I was about done with my coffee. After a couple of days on the Llano his voice wasn't as squally as the last time I'd heard it. But he sure did try to sound tough, I'll give him that.

"Not hardly," Shorty said in a short, clipped voice. "Damn fool thinks I'm forgetful," he said to me. Then, to Temple, he added, "Son, I may be older than dirt but I know good and well that you was here an hour ago and already had you a cup of my coffee. And you know it too. One per man is how I run it, son, and you know that too." That seemed to do it for the conversation between the cook and this troublemaker, at least that was the impression I got from Shorty as he turned back to me. "Speaking of one per man, Chance, I ain't seen your brother yet." Pulling another tin cup out of nowhere, Shorty filled it with coffee and handed it to me. "Why don't you take this out to him?"

"He'll appreciate it, Shorty. Thanks," I said.

"He may appreciate it, Carston, but the sonofabitch don't deserve it, not if you ask me," Temple said, trying to put a growl into his voice and only half succeeding.

"Why don't you shut up and move on?" Shorty said, the testiness in his own voice returning.

Well, hoss, that tore it!

I dismounted, coffee cup still in hand, and gently carried it back to Shorty. Handing it to him, I said, "Hold this for me, will you? I know water's in short supply." He didn't say a word but took the cup then stood back a few steps so it wouldn't get spilled. I reckon he knew what I had in mind.

"I've about had it with you," I said through grit teeth of my own. For all I know, the words might only have been a grumble, but I assure you the feeling was in them.

Temple was still sitting on his mount, but that didn't last long, not long at all. I grabbed him by the shirt and hauled him out of the saddle, an action which thoroughly surprised the man, I do believe. I threw him to the ground like any other bully I've had to tangle with in the past, making sure he landed hard and on his back. Then, when he pushed himself up on his elbows, I hit him hard, right on the jaw, knocking him flat on his back again.

He rolled to his side and scrambled to his feet, facing me in what he took to be a fighting stance. But he was still a mite foggy from being thrown on the ground as hard as he had been, which was all I needed. I stepped into him and hit him hard again with a good right cross, knocking him back against Shorty's chuck wagon. Shorty's boot found Temple's ass and half kicked, half pushed the man back toward me. That was when I hit him hard two more times, a right and left each. This time Shorty stuck his foot out and Temple tripped back over it, the force of my blows sending him falling on his back almost as hard as he'd fallen when I'd pulled him from the saddle.

"What the hell's this?" I heard Charlie Goodnight say in a louder than usual tone of voice. Booming is how it almost sounded. You could tell he was mad right off the bat.

"Old Flannelmouth started cussing Wash Carston," Shorty said. "Started the whole thing, he did. Chance would have killed the bastard with his bare hands ary you hadn't rid up, Charlie."

Charlie threw a glare at Temple, who was getting up and trying to stand straight, still not totally conscious of what was going on about him, I thought. "Is that right, mister?" he snarled. It was plain to see that Charlie Goodnight had no time for this kind of nonsense.

But Temple just glared back at the both of us, trying to figure out who needed it most by my gauge, Goodnight or me. Me, all I did was rub my knuckles, which looked awful raw and felt just as bad as they looked.

"Shorty, give this sorry sonofabitch ten dollars, a canteen of whatever you can spare in the line of water, a day's worth of grub, and his gear," Charlie said to the cook. He'd been glaring back and forth at both Temple and me, so I wasn't all that sure he wasn't talking about me being the one he wanted moving on. But he cleared that up right quick. "Temple, I told you if you started trouble in my camp you wouldn't last the drive. And I meant just what I said." His arm was kind of lazy as he pointed a finger at the man, frowned, and said, "You be out of my camp by sunset. Understand?"

Shorty had a mite of liniment he put on my knuckles before he handed me the cup of now luke-warm coffee. "Don't forget to give this to your brother," he said.

"You bet."

Wash wasn't going to believe what I'd gone through to get him a cup of coffee that afternoon.

So much for family honor.

CHAPTER

★ 11 ★

It was the third night of crossing the Llano Estacado that Charlie Goodnight took what I thought to be an ox bell from the back of the chuck wagon. When he put it on one of the horses in the lead, actually hung it around the horse's neck, I wasn't sure what he had in mind. So I followed him back to the drag, where Oliver Loving and a handful of men who looked almost as petered out as the weaklings they were desperately trying to keep from dropping out were still hard at work.

"Pass it on to the rest of the boys with you back here that I want you to keep a listen out for that ox bell up front," he told Loving and one or two others within earshot. "When you don't think you can hear that lead horse any more, you send one of your riders up to me and I'll hold up the lead steers until you're able to close up the rear to a proper length again."

"Sounds good, Charlie," Loving said with a nod. The man looked about as tired as the rest of us, of that I was sure. But I'll tell you, hoss, he managed to put a pleasing tone to that voice of his as though it were just another day with this herd. And who knew, maybe for this man it was. "I'll pass it on to the men."

The sun had gone down and the stars had appeared, giving us a reasonably clear night by the looks of it. But the heat hadn't let up at all. We'd spent all day roasting in the fires of hell, and although the devil himself may have stopped shoveling the coal and stoking the fires, well, the heat was still there and nothing changed as the sun disappeared from the sky. I found myself muttering to myself, cussing under my breath as the herd moved on. If the weather didn't change, neither did one lone fact—the herd moved on.

Shorty had moved his chuck wagon to the lead of the herd, then pulled up and waited off to the side. I only saw him when he pulled up and came to a halt, for I was on my way to the drag section, where Charlie Goodnight wanted me to give Oliver Loving a hand. Some people have all the luck, I thought as I headed to the drag portion of the drive. It was a good thing I said those words to myself, for if anyone had heard them, I'd likely be eating them by the time us drag riders rode by. Shorty, you see, was handing out another cup of strong black coffee to each and every rider as he passed the chuck wagon.

"I know, don't ask," I said, as the cook handed me a cup of the black stuff.

Shorty nodded in what I took to be a stoic voice. "Now you've got the idea."

"Gracias," Cimarron said as he too rode up beside me and took a grateful cup of coffee from the cook.

"I reckon this kind of weather pretty much suits you," I said to the man, not even sure why I was wasting my breath at that point. Hell, I was even getting tired of cussing the damn fool longhorns, truth to tell. Maybe it was just that I hadn't really seen an awful lot of Cimarron since he'd joined the outfit. But then you don't get to see much of the wranglers who work the remuda for you on a drive like this, that much I'd found out early in the drive.

"Sí," Cimarron replied, taking a sip from his cup. Like me he'd pulled down his bandanna to drink the hot stuff, so I could see his face. What wasn't an olive tint had been browned by time in the sun, enough so that you'd have to hear his accent or take careful note of his dress to really know you were talking to a Mexican.

"Too goddamn hot for my liking," I said and swilled a little coffee around in my mouth before swallowing it. Maybe I could get some of the alkali out from between my teeth before swallowing too much of it killed me. I ran some coffee around in my mouth until it had a brackish taste to it, then spit it out.

Cimarron had a serious look about him as he placed a hand on my forearm and said, "Please, *señor.* Do not mock the Maker about that which He gives you." His eyes took a quick glance upward, as though to indicate he was speaking of the Almighty just in case I didn't know it.

"Mock Him?" I said, not sure what he was getting at. "What's He gonna do, *amigo,* send me to hell? Or did you think this was some kind of picnic we're on here?" I took my John B. off and ran my forearm across my brow, coming away with a sleeve full of sweat, which amazed me since I didn't think I had any sweat left in my body. I shook my head. "No, sir, if there's hell on earth, this is it."

"But this weather is not the only thing He gives you, Chance," Cimarron said, only half smiling. "Perhaps He is testing you, to see if you are worthy of sitting under the cottonwood at the end of the trail. *¿Es verdad?*"

Pa always warned me about arguing politics and religion with a man. It's a sure way to lose a friend or die wondering why you were dying. What had started out as a simple conversation was now turning to a discussion of the Maker. Me, I wasn't having any of it. Not today.

"That's an awful lot of philosophy for a man looks as young as you do," was my reply. I gauged Cimarron to be somewhere between Wash's and my age, although it was hard guessing ages on this frontier. I reckon that old woman they interviewed for the newspaper in Austin hit it right on the head. They asked her what she thought about the frontier. She said it was "hell on horses and women," and I reckon she was right.

"Philosophy does not come with age, *mi amigo,* but with experience," he said.

"Whatever you say, friend."

We both drained the precious little coffee that was left in our tin cups, Cimarron holding his out to me.

"Por favor, please give this to the Short One," he said. I took that to mean Shorty and agreed to with nothing more than a nod.

I watched Cimarron as he left, returning to the remuda. I knew that the word *cimarrón* was Spanish and that the literal translation meant something along the lines of wild or unruly. But I also knew that the

Mexican *vaqueros* used the term to describe an animal that ran alone and would have nothing to do with the rest of its kind, a loner you might say. From what I'd seen so far, Cimarron seemed fairly likable and easy to get along with. As I pulled the bandanna up over my face, I made a mental note to keep the man in mind. He might be worth cultivating as a friend. Hell, a body had damn few of them these days as it was.

According to the dipper, it was somewhere around two o'clock in the morning when we came on Castle Cañon. If what Charlie Goodnight had said was right, this Castle Cañon was a strange looking place during the daylight hours. It had gotten its name because of the fluted cylindrical columns of gray and white stone that stood out from the canyon walls. Most canyons I'd been through might have some jagged rock sticking out here and there, but were otherwise pretty flat from top to bottom. This canyon was just one more wonder of Mother Nature, I reckon.

A sudden breeze came up that felt like a real relief to me, much as I'm sure it did to the rest of the crew. It was gentle, cool, and damp, and for a moment it put us off guard. The longhorns must have smelled that dampness and thought there was water near, for they began to stampede. I reckon it was lucky for us that it was as dark as it was, for those damned cattle couldn't see where they were going any better than those of us trying to keep them under control. But they didn't get far, for Charlie Goodnight, I found out later, had succeeded in holding the leaders to prevent the stampede from going any farther than it did.

At daybreak we were changing horses when I caught up with Charlie.

"Chance, I want you to come with me," he said when he'd remounted. "Where's your brother?"

"Right here," Wash said, an eagerness in his voice as he appeared out of nowhere.

"You get over that woman yet?" Charlie asked, a growl to his own voice.

"Don't worry about the woman," Wash said. He was getting mad. I knew my brother well enough to know when he was getting ready to fight, and this was one of those times. Damn sure betcha!

"I ain't worried about the woman. I'm worried about you. She's not on this cattle drive and you are."

"He can take care of himself, Charlie," I said, stepping in. "You tell him what you need and he'll get it done. Now, what you got in mind?"

"You and Wash and One-Armed Bill and his brother, Charlie, and me are gonna take just over a thousand of these longhorns, the strongest ones in the herd, and see about leading 'em to the water that's supposed to be ahead. As unmanageable as these critters can get, I don't want the whole herd stampeding again like it did last night," he added.

We made a stop at the chuck wagon, where Shorty handed over all of the extra canteens to us. We would fill them once we'd reached the water and get them back to the men as soon as possible. We all knew the urgency behind this, for the men might well be as unmanageable as the cattle if they too got a whiff of the water ahead.

"If I recall right," Charlie said before we left to cut the stronger cattle from the herd, "there's an alkali pond not far from the river we're heading for. I want you to know that if these cattle hit that pond before they get to the river, everything we've done has been for nothing."

"Ain't that the truth," I said, knowing full well that

any animal that drank alkali water was as good as dead.

"You'll have to keep aware of the course of the breeze this morning. Once we know which way it's drifting, we'll be able to make the longhorns strike for the river instead of the pond."

We all nodded our understanding and set to cutting out what looked to be the strongest of the bunch, which turned out to be just over half of the herd.

It was twelve miles to the river, normally enough to make one average day's drive. But once those longhorns got going, they smelled the water in the cool air. Wild is what they got, damn near as desperate as I was feeling, I thought, and off they sped toward the river.

I managed to get in the lead, right alongside of Charlie Goodnight. We stayed in the lead and crossed the river first, Charlie passing off the canteens to Wash, who headed upstream where the water was still clear and took to refilling the bone dry containers. I knew I wouldn't have to keep track of my brother, knew that as soon as he'd filled them he'd ride hell-for-leather back to the outfit and distribute one canteen to each man. Then, and only then, would Wash pull his own canteen out, uncork it, and take a pull on it his own self. Wash was like that.

When the longhorns reached the river, they didn't stop at the bank, and even if they did, the ones in back would have pushed them clean into the river head on. As it was, they all simply pushed the ones to the front of them into the river and wound up being pushed in by the ones behind them before any of them had time to stop and drink the cool blue water. Nor did Charlie and me give them a chance. As soon as they cleared the far banks, we turned them back and they went right back in, finally having a chance to drink as they swam about in the water, most of which was muddy as could be now.

To give you an idea of what kind of volume they crossed in, the force of the herd was such that it impeded the current, causing the waters to back halfway up the banks. Why, you'd have thought the river was reaching a flood stage, it was that high.

Charlie and the Wilson brothers had recrossed the river to the east side, while I had agreed to stay on the west side and catch any strays that might come out of the river and want to roam. However, looking at those hundreds of cattle milling about and getting their fill of water, muddied or not, I didn't think I'd have too many takers. Not today.

Wash had the courtesy to pass by on his way back to the outfit and toss a canteen filled with water my way. I suddenly remembered that with all that water down there in the river, my mouth was still mighty dry. Yes, sir, mighty dry. I took the canteen, undid the cork, and pulled down my bandanna to take a good long pull on the water. I don't mind telling you, hoss, it tasted good, real good. Some of the best liquid I'd ever had run down my gullet.

Then my canteen went flying out of my hand! Just like that! I saw it float through the air, over the bank, and down into the river, landing somewhere between a couple of longhorns. Just before it disappeared I saw what it was that had yanked it out of my hand.

An arrow!

"Son of a bitch," I muttered as I slid out of my saddle and pulled my Colt at the same time. It's a good thing I did too, for another arrow flew through the air where I'd been sitting in my saddle. If I was smart I'd have pulled my Spencer rifle out of its scabbard as I'd dismounted, but my hand was on my Colt first and by the time I was out of the saddle, thinking about that rifle was a mite too late.

Aside from not being able to finish my drink, the first thing that ran through my mind was whether or not Quanah Parker was worth his salt and might not now be shooting at me instead of guaranteeing me safe conduct through the territory.

I was starting to think of how I'd start a stampede and incur the wrath of Charlie Goodnight if I shot my Colt but decided that those longhorns were so taken with the water and drinking it that they'd likely not move for man or earth. So I gave my horse a swat on the rump and watched him skedaddle out of the way rather than get shot.

That was when I saw them. Two of them were running at me, short, squat little men who looked nothing like Comanches, I decided. At the moment, however, I didn't care what they looked like. All I knew was the bastards were trying to kill me. I shot them outright, one shot each to the chest, watching them fall dead, facedown in the dirt.

I would have got the third but my gun jammed. Your throat and lungs weren't the only things the dirt and alkali got into, I was finding out, but it was too late now. I dropped the Colt as the brave ran toward me, a knife in his hand. This one didn't have any bow and arrow, figuring on taking me to the happy hunting grounds with his knife, I reckon. We'd see about that.

I grabbed his wrists as he ran into me and fell backwards, feeling my neck strike the edge of the riverbank and the sharp drop off that was right underneath it. I had damn little time to think, so my instincts and reflexes took over. I kicked my legs up, pushing the warrior up with them, I hoped. When the bottom part of his body went up, I pushed off the wrists I had hold of and he went over me and off into the river or river embankment, whichever was directly below me.

I didn't have time to look to see what had happened to him. I only had time to look in the direction he had come from, only to see a handful of his friends coming toward me to replace him. I was dead and I knew it. All I could do was cuss and pray. Still, I had the bowie knife at my side, the weapon I'd nearly forgotten about. I was reaching for it to make a last effort to keep my hair from getting lifted when I heard a half dozen shots ring out from the eastern bank of the river.

I rolled half over and immediately saw Charlie Goodnight and the Wilson brothers, each with a rifle in his hands, shooting at the charging warriors as though they were so many targets and this was target practice. When I rolled back to look at the damage they'd done, I saw that it was considerable. The three who had been charging my way were flat on their face as the first two I'd shot. Not a one of them moved either, so I knew that Goodnight and the Wilson boys had been true in their aim.

Whatever other Indians had been with these raiders had suddenly disappeared. They'd come and gone, just as I'd known the Comanche would.

As for the cattle, they didn't move a bit. Not an inch. All except for the longhorn who had a warrior stuck on the end of one of his horns and was wagging his head back and forth, trying to rid himself of the heavy object impaled on it, I reckon. I could only assume this was the warrior I'd thrown over my head and past me into the river.

Charlie Goodnight was making his way across the river toward my side. As he did I picked up my Colt and began studying one of the warriors on the ground. All I needed was one look to know that Quanah Parker had kept his word. These fellows were Apaches, likely Mescalero or Lipan, I couldn't make out which. They were not, however, Comanche.

"You all right?" Charlie Goodnight said, as his horse made it up and over the riverbank. I thought I noted a bit of concern in his voice.

"What took you so long?" I asked, a scowl of my own on my face as I spoke. "These bastards could have killed me."

Charlie Goodnight didn't say a word.

I could only hope that in that moment he was learning something about Chance Carston and the way I operated.

CHAPTER

★ 12 ★

As soon as Charlie Goodnight thought the longhorns had gotten their fill of water, he put them to graze. It was Charlie Wilson, One-Armed Bill Wilson's brother, who he put in charge of them, with instructions to hold them while they grazed and not let them back into the water for a while.

I reckon Charlie Goodnight knew that he wasn't the only man who'd been pushing these longhorns for three full days and in want of sleep, for he dug into his pocket and produced a watch. Handing it to Charlie Wilson, he said, "Charlie, you take this watch and let the men sleep ten or fifteen minutes at a time, one and then the other, but for your life don't go to sleep yourself."

I could have fallen asleep then and there, I reckon,

but Charlie said he was going to help the men on drag bring in the rest of the herd, so I figured I'd tag along with him and get my rest later, when the entire herd was at the Pecos River.

"Aw, hell," he said on our way back to the drag, riding at a gentle lope. I gave a quick glance in the direction he was looking and soon followed him, chasing about half a dozen cows on their way to water again. Apparently, Wilson and whoever might have been watching the herd had fallen asleep, for no one was making a try at stopping these cows except for Charlie Goodnight and me.

The trouble was they weren't headed for the river, which wouldn't have been much more than a matter of diverting them back to the grazing area. Not these fools. They'd taken off for one of the alkali ponds Charlie had described as being so deadly. Three had finished drinking from the pond by the time we reached them, but it was too late. Turning away from the water, one after another of them dropped in her tracks and died on the spot. As for the other three, it was only a matter of minutes before they were dead too. That's how poisonous that alkali water was.

Oliver Loving had everything as much in hand as could be by the time we reached the rest of the herd. A quick glance told me we might have just over five hundred head left.

The rest of the crew looked a whole lot more lively than when we'd left them that morning, a fact that likely owed to Wash's getting back with a fresh canteen of water for everyone. It was too bad I couldn't say the same for the longhorns they were pushing. Damn near every one of them looked like they were ready to drop.

If having a pull or two on a canteen of water did

wonders for our crew, the smell of water from the river once we got the herd moving toward the Pecos just have done the same thing for the cattle. As soon as they smelled the water they became as unmanageable as the first half of the herd had that morning. Suddenly, they were crazy for water, and I do believe that if we had placed every jack man of the crew on one side of the herd, why, the lot of them wouldn't have been able to budge those longhorns! They were a determined bunch and water was what they were heading for.

"Charlie and me found an alkali pond off on the right," I told Oliver Loving, who was bringing up the rear, as usual. "There's a couple more of 'em on the far side of the Pecos. I'd post a man or two by 'em to make sure we don't lose any more cattle than we already have," I added, relating what Charlie and I had seen at the alkali hole on the west side of the Pecos not an hour ago. I reckon it was that story that got Loving to action, maybe because some of these cattle were his.

The point of the Pecos River we were headed for was almost like a ditch, the banks being somewhere between six and ten feet high, as I recalled. When the longhorns, that seemed to get crazier with each step toward the river, reached the drop off it didn't even faze them. Not a one of them halted, plunging into the river one after another, one on top of another, much like the stronger ones had earlier. The remuda was bringing up the rear and was just as thirsty as the longhorns, following the remainder of the herd into the river.

A fair amount of those cattle that were trampled over wound up drowning in the Pecos. Some, on the other hand, found dangerous footing on the rather sharp cut banks and set to taking in water. Still others drifted off into a bend in the river that turned out to be filled with quicksand.

"Over here!" Charlie Goodnight yelled and soon had half the crew working with him in an effort to try to pull out those longhorns stuck in the quicksand bottom. Every one of us had a rope out, each tossed around one of the cattle and its horns. I'll tell you, hoss, you've never seen so many horses backing up at one time, not unless you've been to a circus of late. But try as we might, we couldn't get but a handful of those steers out of the quicksand and most of them wound up going under. Finally, we rode off, leaving upwards of a hundred longhorns hopelessly stranded in that quicksand.

"How many cattle you figure we've lost so far?" I asked Charlie shortly afterward, both of us taking a well-deserved break and a sip of water.

"I don't know," he said in a dejected manner. In a way it was unlike Charlie Goodnight, for he was usually full of life and orders and things to do and pointing out who should be doing them. Now, for the first time, it seemed to me, I was seeing the sad and lonely side of the man, the side likely hidden to most of us. Did I catch him in a weak moment? Who could tell? Whether it was or not, I had no intention of pursuing it with the man. Hell, I was tired enough to sleep a week and I wanted to be around when I woke up, not one of the ornaments on a longhorn's rack, like that Apache I'd fought this morning. "Three hundred would be an educated man's guess."

I nodded in agreement. This wasn't the time to argue with the man, of that I was sure.

"The Pecos," he growled in a tone as poisonous as the alkali ponds in the area. *"The graveyard of the*

cowman's hopes. I hate it! It's as treacherous as the goddamn Indians themselves." At first he'd been looking at the Pecos River, of which he was speaking. But by the time his words were out, his gaze had drifted to the east, the direction we'd come from and the three hundred head of cattle that were left behind as markers to those who would follow, markers that clearly let it be known that only a fool would try to make this crossing.

Like I said, it wasn't a time to argue anything with the man.

"Anything you say, boss, anything you say."

"Anything you say, ma'am," Dallas Bodeen was saying to Margaret Ferris as he finished a late lunch at the community table in the Ferris House, Twin Rifles' one and only boardinghouse. "I'll have you plenty of firewood for your evening meal, Miss Margaret. Don't you fret none at all about it."

Tall and weathered, the big man wore buckskins from top to bottom, a feature that seemed to be dying out in the more civilized areas of the west, specifically the towns. If Dallas Bodeen resembled a onetime mountain man it was because he was. Like Will Carston, he had spent his earlier years in the Rocky Mountains as a free trapper. In fact, it was during those early years that he had first encountered Will Carston and the two had formed a fast friendship that was still as solid as the day they'd met. When the beaver trade had petered out, the two men had gone on to become Texas Rangers together. It wasn't long ago that the two, along with two other friends who were former rangers, had made a trek to Austin to try to reform the rangers. Back from their mission, Dallas Bodeen had decided to stay on in Twin Rifles and struck the same deal with Margaret Ferris that Will Carston had—chop a day's worth of deadwood for boarding and meals.

"Yes, ma'am, you'll have plenty of firewood," Dallas was adding when Sarah Ann walked through the door to the Ferris House. All attention seemed to fall on her now, perhaps because of the worried look she had about her. "Well now, Miss Sarah Ann, you sure do look a mite peaked," Dallas said at the sight of her. "Why don't you have a seat here."

"Yes, Sarah Ann, please do," Margaret said, a tone of concern in her voice. "Let me get you some water."

Dallas Bodeen had long been without his wife and daughter, who had been killed by the Comanche some years back, so he was all too aware of how lacking in manners he was with womenfolk. Still, it seemed as though he should say something while the blond young woman sat there with a pitiful look on her face.

"It ain't that hot out, is it?" he finally blurted out, immediately regretting it. "I'm sorry, ma'am, I—"

"Never mind, Mr. Bodeen," Margaret said, marching back into the room with a glass of water, which she handed over to Sarah Ann. "You can start chopping that wood for me now, if you don't mind."

"Oh! Yes, ma'am. I'll do that." He gathered up his old beaver hat from the hat tree in the corner of the room. He sloshed it on and gave Sarah Ann one more worried glance before silently leaving the room for the axe and the deadwood out back.

"Now, child, you tell me what's the matter," Margaret said, addressing her friend as though she were her own daughter.

"Oh, I don't know," Sarah Ann said in a distraught voice, her lip quivering. "Papa says I haven't got my mind on my work. I got two orders mixed up at the noon meal and he told me to go take a walk to clear my head." She paused, the distress in her tone suddenly turning to sorrow as she looked deep into Margaret Ferris's eyes. Then tears burst forth as she said, "Papa raised his voice to me."

Then she was on her feet and burying her face in Margaret's shoulder as the older woman held her tight, once again as though she were her own daughter. After the crying died down, Margaret took the girl by her shoulders and held her away from her, a smile coming to her face as she did.

"It's not your papa that's got you daydreaming, my dear, that's for sure," she said in a tender, motherly voice. "It's Wash, isn't it?"

"Yes," Sarah Ann said, sounding almost embarrassed as she spoke the words. "I guess it is."

"You say Big John raised his voice to you?"

"Yes. It's the first time in a long while that he's ever really gotten mad at me, Margaret. It scared me." She was silent for a moment before adding, "I miss him so." Margaret didn't have to ask to know her focus had changed from her father to her new husband. "I wish I knew *where* he was. *How* he was. I'm so worried about him."

"I know, Sarah Ann," Margaret said, placing a hand on Sarah Ann's as though it would comfort her more. "But you have to remember that it was that way before you got married and it will likely be that way most of your lives. Men like Wash and Will and Chance are always going off to prove something to themselves or somebody else. Believe me, I know how you feel for I've felt the same way about Will myself. Don't you worry, they'll be back. All of those Carston men will be back."

"Yes," Sarah Ann said, a sigh of relief in her voice

now. It wasn't that she didn't know Wash would be back, she just needed to hear it from someone. She found herself feeling glad she had come to Margaret Ferris. She seemed to have an answer for everything.

"Oh, there you are." The booming sound came from the doorway and it was Big John Porter, Sarah Ann's father, who filled out the frame. He still had a bloody meat cleaver in his hand, looking as though he had been interrupted doing his work. "Look, I—" he started to say, probably in some rare form of apology, for he looked about as bad as Sarah Ann had when she walked into the Ferris House. He never did get a chance to finish though.

"You!" Margaret said in outrage, suddenly on her feet and approaching the man.

"What?" That one word had totally confused Big John.

"How dare you raise your voice to this child." Margaret Ferris was clearly on the warpath, of that Big John was certain. And doing it in an even voice. But she'd planted her hands on her hips, much like he had at one time or another, meaning to be heard if nothing else. "Why, I've a good notion to take that cleaver out of your hand and split your skull wide open, you big bully! And let me tell you something else, John Porter. If I ever hear of you doing this again to Sarah Ann, why, I'll . . . I'll do just that, by God!"

Big John Porter looked as though he had been kicked in the belly and didn't know how to breathe anymore, the look of surprise on his face was that great.

"Now you get back to the cafe of yours and tend to it," she added, still very much in control of the situation. "Sarah Ann and I are having some afternoon tea and she'll be back . . . well, she'll be back when she's good and ready." Margaret Ferris then grabbed Big John Porter by the arm and physically turned him around and pushed him out the door and back toward his own establishment. She was watching him go, a dazed look on him as he slowly shook his head, when she heard some clapping behind her. She turned to see Dallas Bodeen standing in the back entrance to the kitchen.

"You know, Miss Margaret, I ain't never seen anyone in this town back talk to that man before," Dallas said with a grin. "Ary you're running for sheriff of this county, why, you've got my vote. Yes, ma'am."

"I thought you were chopping wood." Margaret Ferris still had a touch of annoyance in her voice.

"Oh, I am, ma'am." He held up a glass of water in one hand. "A body does get thirsty though."

Although the one-sided exchange between Big John Porter and Margaret Ferris had been humorous, Dallas thought he still saw a touch of worry in Sarah Ann's eyes. He made his way over to the community table and took a seat across from Sarah Ann.

"Tell me something, Missy. Did Wash ever tell you about our exploits on the way up to Austin last year?" Dallas asked, taking a sip of water.

"No. He doesn't talk much about himself."

"Yeah. That's his style. It's Chance who's the loud-mouth."

Sarah Ann forced a smile. "Yes, he can be that."

"Then he didn't tell you how he saved our lives, did he?" Dallas said, cocking an eye toward the young lady.

"He did?" The fact seemed to bewilder her.

"Well, Miss Sarah Ann, it was like this," Dallas said and told her of the day Will and Dallas had ridden up to Joe Quintana's place, being chased by Comanches.

They'd slid off their horses and begun shooting back at the renegades right out in the open with hardly any cover about at all. It was a wonder they hadn't been killed on the spot.

"Then our guns was empty," Dallas said. "Empty as the Rio Grande on the Fourth of July." A wild look came into his eyes as he spoke. He took another sip of water before saying, "Now, this is where old Jim Bridger would tell you that them Injuns killed him once they got him surrounded. But I ain't gonna do that."

He studied the glass of water now nearly gone, knowing the silence itself would build the tension he was looking for. After a minute of it, Sarah Ann could stand it no longer.

"Well, what happened!" she said in an exasperated voice.

"Why, Wash saved us. Yes, ma'am. There he comes a-riding out of nowhere. 'Fill your hands you sonsa—' Well, you know what he meant," Dallas continued. "Puts the reins of his horse in his mouth and charges the lot of 'em. Had his pistol in one hand and that Colt revolving rifle in the other. And let me tell you, Missy, ary he didn't kill a whole lot of 'em, he sure did make 'em think the United States Cavalry had arrived!" Dallas gave the woman a wink and a nod, an indication that the story had come to an end.

"Really? Wash did all of that?" Sarah Ann asked in awe.

"Well, I don't know about putting the reins in his mouth, but that's basically the same story Will told me," Margaret said in agreement. She also handed Dallas a second glass of water, likely knowing that storytelling gives men like Dallas Bodeen a keen thirst.

"Thank you, ma'am," Dallas said and downed the water in one big gulp. He stood up.

"Thanks, Dallas. Thanks for telling me that story," Sarah Ann said. Dallas thought he saw a more chipper look on her face now. Maybe he hadn't lost his touch with the women after all.

"I figured you'd like it." The big man put the empty glass on the table and placed his hands on Sarah Ann's shoulders as she got up from the community table. "Now you get back there and do your job the way you're supposed to and save your daydreaming until your husband gets back."

She silently walked to the door, ready to follow his advice.

"Sarah Ann."

"Yes, Dallas," she said over her shoulder.

"You ask me, old Wash is gonna make a habit out of saving the hides of all the rest of us." Dallas smiled at her.

"Yes," Sarah said, returning the smile. "I do believe you're right."

As he watched Sarah Ann leave, Dallas Bodeen somehow knew he'd made a firm believer of Sarah Ann.

CHAPTER

★ 13 ★

It took three days to get the men, horses, and cattle rested up enough to move on again. Not that you could blame any of the three, for the crossing we'd made of the Llano Estacado was one to tell your grandchildren about.

As for the Pecos country itself, well, hoss, it had to be some of the most desolate land I'd ever come across in my life. Mind you now, I'll be the first to admit that the river was full of fish, and for a day or so they even tasted good. Hell, you'd say the same thing after damn near a month of eating boiled beef and beans. I guarantee it! But other than the fish, you couldn't spot a living thing in the area, not even birds . . . or those goddamn wolves that we'd had trouble with before striking out across the Llano Estacado. Either the earth had swallowed them up whole, or they'd had the good sense to know when to get out of the area. Which meant that eighteen lonely cowhands and two thousand some longhorns were the only ones crazy enough to cross this infernal land. The only thing there seemed to be one hell of a lot of was heat.

And rattlesnakes.

Jesus, Mary, and Joseph, they were everywhere! The trouble we had from them once we moved out made handling these longhorns seem like a pure joy, believe me. Why, there was so many of them you couldn't believe your eyes. Shoot, Cross-eyed Nate Brauner managed to kill every snake he saw, and he had the worst sight of anyone on the crew! That's how many rattlesnakes there were. Actually, being cross-eyed like that was an advantage for Nate, for the man could both watch the herd and shoot at snakes at the same time.

"How many you figure he's got now?" I asked Shorty one day as Nate rode away from the chuck wagon.

Shorty pulled back the flap of his wagon and gave a quick furtive glance inside. "Seventy at last count," he said. "But old Nate's gonna have to stop pretty soon. He's gathered up more snake skins and rattles than I can carry. Hell, I hit one more bump and them rattles are gonna scare my team clean out of the territory," he added and went back to work.

"By the way, Cookie, what's on the menu for supper tonight?" I said before departing. "Whatever it was you had last night wasn't half bad."

"You're in luck then, my friend," he said with a lopsided grin on his face. Somehow, I got the notion he was enjoying this more than I was. "Same thing's on the menu for tonight."

"I didn't know there was that many jackrabbits in the country," I said, starting to feel a might puzzled about this conversation. No one had complained about the supper meal the night before, and although they didn't, I wasn't about to say anything to get the crew started on it. Besides, the meat did taste a lot like rabbit to me.

"Well now, mister, I ain't seen a jackrabbit in the last hundred miles, truth to tell," Shorty said, a smile that can only be described as conniving on his mug.

"Then what in the hell did we have last night?"

Shorty pulled back the wagon cover and gave that same shifty glance inside as he had when I'd questioned him about Cross-eyed Nate's rattlesnakes. "Fricassee rattlesnake," he said the way a man does when he knows he's going to have the last laugh.

I didn't say a damn thing, just pulled the reins on my mount as I felt the bile rise in my stomach. Truth to tell, hoss, as strong as I like to believe I am, I did feel a mite queasy over last night's supper.

CHAPTER
★ 14 ★

It was Horsehead Crossing we had come upon when we at last reached the Pecos River. But after three days of continuous riding across the Llano Estacado, why, I don't think anyone of us noticed, least of all me. So it wasn't until we were leaving that I really took notice of it.

One thing about the people out here who pass out names; they're usually to the point, although sometimes downright funny, if you get my drift. I reckon the best example of that is a location Pa had come across way back when, in his days as a mountain man. The official designation of the two pointed peaks that bordered the canyon was Twin Peaks. But the old mountain men, well, like I say, they get kind of raucous at times. So being the men that they were, they referred to the landmark as Two Tits. I reckon you had to see it from afar to look on it as what I'll just call the healthier part of a woman.

Horsehead Crossing had been given an appropriate moniker, although there didn't seem to be a damn thing about it that was comical at all. No, sir. The skeletons of horses and mules could be found on the banks of both shores of the Pecos at this location. According to Charlie, this was the first water hole north of Chihuahua, which was a good sixty miles. It was a good thing we weren't heading south, because I didn't think I could stand that much more distance between me and water again, not after the Llano!

"If I recall right," Charlie said that day as the herd moved out, "both the Comanche and the Apache would raid into Old Mexico and come back with a fair amount of horses, driving 'em as hard as they could till they reached Horsehead. Most times they made the mistake of running 'em clean into the river and letting 'em drink till they got sick and died."

"I'm surprised our cattle didn't do that," I said with a wry smile.

"Hell, them longhorns was pretty tough when we rounded 'em up, Chance," he said, smiling right back at me, the occasional grin I hadn't seen in some time suddenly reappearing on the man's face. "I figured that if them critters could make it across a hundred miles of staked plains, why, they must be *mean* to boot, so I let 'em drink their fill." With a wink and a nod, he added, "Looks like I was right."

In the back of my mind was the sure knowledge that those half dozen longhorns who'd fallen dead as soon as they tasted that alkali pond didn't appear to be so tough. But Charlie was the boss; besides, I knew the gist of what he was talking about and had no desire to argue with the man.

Charlie Goodnight seemed to know a whole lot about Horsehead Crossing, a lot more than I did anyway. Old "Rip" Ford had been over the trail back in '49, looking for a practical wagon route to El Paso. But it seems it was a John R. Bartlett, who'd been surveying the Mexican boundary in 1850, who had given the location the name it now carried.

We followed the Pecos north, sticking to the east side of the river. Aside from all of those rattlesnakes, I don't think a one of the crew bellyached. Mostly it was because we had water right close at hand if a man every wanted to refill his canteen on the spur of the moment. I reckon you do a lot of rethinking on things after you've gone across something like the Llano. Hell, you can't help but do that.

I was about to ask Charlie why we hadn't crossed at Horsehead when it came to mind that it was on the west side of the river that I'd had my run-in with the Apaches. All we had to do was stay a ways to the east of the Pecos and it seemed likely that we wouldn't have any trouble from them. And if we did, they'd have to make one hell of a lot of noise crossing that river to get to us first, all of which would give us plenty of time to shoot them out of their saddles. In a strange sort of way it made sense, for Quanah Parker seemed to have taken my request for safe conduct through his land in a serious manner. I hadn't seen a Comanche since that day I'd done my palavering with the man, all of which made me feel a lot safer. Not that I didn't think I saw some eerie things those three days on the Llano. Heat like that could put a lot of things in a man's eyes, not to mention his mind.

"What's on the menu tonight, Cookie?" Emmett asked as he finished another cup of coffee one day at noon camp.

Shorty Hall pushed his hat back and scratched his head as though indecisive about the answer he should give.

"Well, Mr. Horseman, it's like this," he said. "I'm waiting to see what Cross-eyed Nate brings in today. Ary he makes his quota, why, I'll gladly make your favorite." To stifle any doubt about what he was referring to, Shorty reached over and pulled back the flap on his chuck wagon, just as he had with me a while back.

All of a sudden, Emmett and a good share of the other men within hearing range were quick to toss their tin cups into the general range of Shorty and make a hasty retreat back to the herd. Word had gotten around quickly about Shorty's fricassee rattlesnake recipe. Some had mistook it for fish, while others, like me, had taken it for rabbit. I do believe that the only reason we'd eaten the damned stuff was the fact that it was the only food being served within a hundred miles and we were each hungry as a grizzly that's just come out of hibernation. And that's a powerful appetite if you think about it. For the most part none of us complained when Shorty served the boiled beef and beans again. Nary a one.

Pope's Crossing was where we crossed the Pecos to the west side of the river. Like Horsehead Crossing, Pope's was one of the few crossings along the several hundred miles the Pecos River ran.

"Depending on which one of them surveyors you believe, Pope's Crossing is close to the Texas and New Mexico Territory border," Charlie said. If that was true, I sure didn't see any markers up that bragged about it. But then that was how this land was.

It was a Captain John Pope who had crossed here as he made a preliminary survey for one of the first Pacific railways back in the early '50s, Charlie said. That all sounded fashionable enough to me. It was when Charlie added the rather strange fact that this man had returned here and dug a well not far away that I got to wondering if he wasn't some relative of those Spanish conquistadors. Where those Spaniards had been searching for the fountain of youth, this Pope fellow was looking for some kind of strange water that sounded just as bad. Artesian, Charlie said it was. Naturally, I couldn't do much more than shake my head when I finished listening to Charlie.

"Don't believe me, do you, Chance?" he said.

"It ain't that, Charlie. It's just that I always figured cool, clear water was good enough for me," I said with raised eyebrows. "I reckon I never did trust anything with a foreign moniker to it. That's what Pa said way back when."

"Your Pa taught you right, Chance," Charlie replied. "Like I said, he sounds like a good man."

I found myself wanting to think old Charlie was saying those things about Pa because he meant them, but it seemed likely he was saying them because he knew that Pa had been a Texas Ranger, just like Wash and me. And I had a notion there was a big difference.

We spent the better part of the afternoon getting the herd across the Pecos to the west side. Shorty had found a shallow enough place to get across and set up camp for the night while we worked that herd of longhorns across the water. They didn't seem so eager to stay in the water now, not since having their ready fill of the wet stuff on a daily basis again. If that was a relief for the longhorns, I can guarantee you that I for one felt a real surge of relief upon hearing word passed back to us that there were no rattlesnakes on the western side of the river. Or at least nothing like we'd encountered on the east side of the river. It was almost as though the horses we were riding could sense it too, for they appeared to have a liveliness about them.

But Emmett's remuda, well, that was a different story. The man could only shrug when I asked him what was making them so skittish now.

"Beats the hell outta me," was all he could conjure up. "How about you, Wash? Any idea?"

"Nope. I don't recall seeing much of nothing like it before, truth to tell." Wash had taken hold of himself ever since we'd come across the Llano Estacado. Although he didn't say so, it was almost as though Wash had faced all of his troubles in those three hot, frustrating days and buried himself in work. If that was what had happened, which was indeed what Emmett had told me in an aside, it had helped him concentrate on the job at hand. It made me feel better about him, made me realize I had one less worry to fret over.

"It's the Indian," Cimarron said, abruptly taking part in the conversation. It wasn't as though he had been asked. I reckon we were just three white men who'd struck up a debate and had totally ignored him. "The horses smell the Indian. He is near." He shrugged. "Sometimes the cattle, they smell him too."

"I'll keep that in mind," I said, although for the life of me I couldn't spot anything on the far bank except the crew and the cattle milling about.

"Wash, why don't you give me a hand with the far side of the remuda," Emmett said. "Let these two yahoos watch this side."

I didn't know whether Emmett was reading my mind or what, but I'd found myself wanting to talk to Cimarron again, preferably alone. Maybe it was the fact that we'd all but shunned the man in our conversation. Or maybe it was wanting to make a true friend out of him. Like I said, friends are hard to come by. Real hard to come by.

"I'd bet a dollar you've been on the run," I said to him when Emmett and my brother were gone. Not that I'm a great conversationalist, you understand. Hell, I don't even know if that's the right word for it. I just ain't as good with words as Pa or Wash are. But give me a Colt or a Spencer . . .

"What makes you say that, *amigo?*" Cimarron said with a half smile. At least he had what I took to be a sense of humor, I'll give him that.

I tried smiling back. "Oh, I got to thinking about all that philosophy you were throwing around back on the Llano. If experience is what you've got to have, I'd say you've been around a mite."

"True." The smile was still on his lips, but I thought I saw a hint of it in his eyes now too.

"Give some thought to what you said, I did. You know, about mocking and all." Not that I'd really done it, you understand. Hell, I never was much of a churchgoer. It just seemed like a good way to pay him a compliment. Or maybe make a friend.

"If you gave my words thought, then perhaps they meant little to you, *mi amigo,*" he said. The smile was gone, the look on his face closer to serious than anything. When I didn't reply, he added, "This morning you were on *muy* profane terms with the Maker."

My smile suddenly turned sheepish. "It's a hard habit to break." I had to look away, at once ashamed of what I'd said. It was a weak excuse if ever there was one. Pa would say that, of that I was sure. "Look," I said, jerking my head around and forcing myself to look the man in the eye as I spoke. "All I wanted to do was be your friend, Cimarron. Sorry. I didn't mean to lie to you."

"*Amigos* should never lie to one another," he said. "For a true *amigo,* I believe it is a cardinal sin."

"I reckon you're right." Whoever this man's parents were, they had taught him well, taught him from the Good Book most likely. And it had stuck, that was evident too.

After a bit of awkward silence, the corner of Cimarron's lip curled up a mite and he said, "Come, *amigo,* Señor Emmett is right. The herd becomes restless." He was right, the remuda had become more skittish as we talked, particularly on our side. So I followed the man as he rode off, helping him out where I could, although he was much better at working a herd of horses than I was. I'd be the first to admit it. But somehow it didn't matter to me. Me, who was usually so hardheaded at being right about things. At first I couldn't figure it out, not at all. Then it hit me and I knew.

Cimarron had called me *amigo* as he'd ridden off to calm the herd. And by God, I do believe he meant it!

The remuda was the last group to cross the river. By the time that took place, Emmett, Wash, Cimarron, and I were starting to have a whole lot of trouble with the horses. I didn't know how seriously Emmett and my brother had taken this Mexican outcast at his suggestion that the horses could smell the Indians and that this was what had caused them to become edgy, but I was beginning to take a whole lot of stock in it. Not that I could see Indians on the far shore, you understand. But sometimes you take your gut instinct and trust to its truth. And if you put any faith in your mount, why, you'll do the same with him too.

We didn't lose any horses crossing the Pecos, but it sure did seem like we played hell with them that last twenty feet to the shore. I gave Emmett a hard glare, the kind that demands an answer, as we crossed, but the big man couldn't do much more than shrug as he had before. I'd have tried making eye contact with Cimarron, but he was already on the bank, herding the horses off to the side and into a clearing as they wandered ashore.

"Looks like them horses wore you fellers out more than the longhorns did the rest of the crew," Shorty said, handing Emmett, Wash, and me a quick cup of coffee after we'd taken care of the remuda. Cimarron had decided to stay with the herd, still convinced that it was Indians the remuda had smelled.

"I'd like to see you get out there and herd them mustangs, friend," Emmett said in all but a snarl. He could sound almost as vicious as Shorty when the subject of food preparation came up, if you know what I mean.

"Mr. Horseman, you'd be surprised what I've done in my lifetime," Shorty said with a snort, but all it drew was a derisive laugh from the ex-sergeant.

I'd only taken one full swallow of coffee when I heard a thud off in the distance, followed by a sharp cry of pain. All of us looked about the same time to see Cimarron falling off his horse, a surefire arrow sticking in his side as he fell.

The first thing that crossed my mind was already taking place as I had my Colt in my hand, more out of force of habit than anything else. But that was as far as it went, for I knew that if I fired at the Apache I spotted not far from Cimarron, why, the whole herd would be in a stampede in no time. Still, the son of a bitch was about to steal our horses, if my guess was right, and something had to be done about it.

"Dig out that goddamn bow and arrow of mine," I ordered Shorty as I dropped my coffee cup and ran toward Cimarron and the Apache, so far the only one I'd spotted. Keep in mind that my Colt was still in hand. If it came down to it, I'd rather lose my job more than my life.

Cimarron was on his feet before I could get there to give him any assistance. I didn't know if anyone else was following me, but I'll tell you, hoss, I sure was praying hard that someone was, for when I saw a couple more of that Apache's friends show up out of nowhere . . . well, I felt awful lonesome awful quick.

One of them came at me in a rush, a knife in his hand. But if I couldn't fire that Colt of mine, I'd damn sure make good use of it as a club. I brought the barrel of the six-gun down on the heathen's head, knocking him aside. As I did, his knife cut a wide swath at me and I felt my side get warm with what I suddenly knew was my own blood. And the strangest thing happened just then. That same Apache, the one who'd cut me, got hit by an arrow, a Comanche arrow at that! A look of anguish and pain crossed his face as the arrow sank into his side and then he sank to the ground. It was almost as though the arrow had struck a vital organ in the man, for he surely did look dead by the time he was laying on the ground. Somehow I knew in that instant it was Shorty Hall who'd fired that arrow.

Out of the corner of my eye I saw both Wash and Emmett tackling the two other Apaches, a sight which made me feel real good again, being bloodied or not. I knew Wash and Emmett would take care of them one way or another, but the next time I glanced that way, why, both of those Apaches had Comanche arrows sticking out of them too!

It was Cimarron I'd come to help, but I needn't have. Besides, I was too late. By the time I'd reached him, that Apache he was mixing with had driven a knife into the Mexican's stomach and was twisting it about for effect. But Cimarron wasn't giving up, not yet. He'd pulled a Colt navy from his holster and was fixing to do in the Apache with his last breath, I reckon. But in that one moment he must have remembered what firing his pistol would do to the herd, not to mention the horses. Suddenly, he grabbed the short little Apache by the neck and pulled him to his own body. It was then and only then that he stuck the navy six-gun in between them, the barrel right up against the Apache's body, his own right in front of it, and pulled the trigger. The six-gun being right in between the two bodies, the shot was muffled for the most part and I doubt if the horses or the longhorns heard it at all. But by God, that Apache felt it, I can guarantee you that. His body was jolted back and I swear a chunk of the side of his back came flying out. He looked a hell of a lot worse in death than Cimarron did.

Both men fell to the ground then in their dying moments. But it was Cimarron I took in my arms. If I could have killed the Apache all over again, believe me, I'd have done it!

"You take it easy now, pard, and we'll fix you right up," I said to him. "Shorty, get the hell over here and bring your medicinals!" I yelled, not caring who heard me.

Cimarron's face moved back and forth in one slow, long movement. "No, *amigo,*" he said. "Friends

should not lie to one another, remember? It is a sin."
You'd swear he had a contented feeling, the way he
spoke, but I knew he must have been in one hell of a
lot of pain from those two wounds.

Still, I felt like I was in more pain than the man in
my arms. Or maybe it was the sudden realization that
I was about to lose a friend I'd just made. All I knew
was that if you told me that lump in my throat was my
heart, why, I'd have believed you, hoss. I really would.
That's what it felt like.

"I forgot, *amigo*, it's a sin." I wanted to cry in the
worst way. But I didn't. All I could do was look into
this lad's eyes and know that I couldn't save him, that
like it or not I was losing him.

Then his hand was on my arm and I felt a gentle
squeeze, as though he were letting me know he was
still here. "I am no longer on the run," Cimarron said,
and then he died.

There was a long silence before I felt another hand
take hold of my shoulder and give it a firm grip.

"He died the way a man should, Chance," Emmett
said in a sincere voice. "With his friends."

I put that on the wooden cross we left at the head of
his grave. If nothing else, I wanted Cimarron to always
know that he had died among his friends.

CHAPTER
★ 15 ★

I would have buried Cimarron myself but the pain in my side had grown considerably. Or maybe it was the loss of blood that took the energy out of me. At any rate, it was Wash and Emmett who did most of the digging while I set to work on the wooden headstone for the grave. But first I'd been subjected to Shorty and his medicinals and was barely able to breathe once the cook was through with me. The cut that Apache had given me hadn't been all that deep, although you'd have thought so by the amount of blood I'd lost. Shorty had me remove my shirt, then poured what he called a slosh of his medicinal alcohol into one of those tin cups. At first I figured he was going to give it to me to drink, but the damn fool had no such a thing in mind. He tossed it on my wound. It was then I realized why he had me take a good hold of my bowie knife with my teeth. Of course, by the time I took it out of my mouth, I thought I'd left a good healthy imprint on the knife as well.

"Damn but that hurt!" I all but yelled at the cook, who now had a satisfying look about him. I don't mind telling you it was a look I didn't like.

"Ain't as tough as Bridger, are you?" he snorted with the same satisfaction that had accompanied his smile.

"Bridger? What the hell are you talking about?" At first I hadn't the foggiest idea what the man was talking about. Or had he snuck himself a nip of that grain alcohol before pouring a cup of it to toss on me?

"Told you I'd been a few places and done a few things."

"Is that a fact," I said, making sure I sounded less than interested, although the tone in his voice had a mite of the brag to it and I knew he was talking with a good deal of pride, no matter what it was about.

"You sure are awful slow, boy," he said as he continued to bandage my side. I could only assume that the silence between us was meant to give me time to think. So I did.

I knew for a fact that men like Shorty Hall had held down more than one job in their lifetime. Hell, old cusses like this were too damned old not to have held more than one job. Take Pa, for example. He'd spent most of his youth in the Rocky Mountains as a mountain man. It was then that I made the connection. Not between Pa and Shorty, you understand, so much as it was between the mountain men and the name Bridger that Shorty had just thrown out to me. It now became obvious that he had meant Jim Bridger, one of the premier mountain men, if you listened to Pa talk about those times.

I suddenly understood the comment Shorty had made about not being as tough as Bridger too. Hell, I'd heard Pa tell the story many a time. It was back in the summer of 1835, during the rendezvous of that season, that a young doctor from back east by the name of Marcus Whitman had stopped off at the rendezvous momentarily on his way to Oregon to see how fertile the land up that way was. Being a doctor, he'd taken a fascination with Jim Bridger, a tall muscular mountain man who claimed he had an arrowhead in his back and that it had been there for the better part of two years. Even then Bridger was known for being quite a liar with his stories, so the doctor named Whitman had to see for himself. He probed about Bridger's body and did indeed find the arrowhead the mountain man said he had buried in him. In a total state of disbelief, he'd told Bridger that having an arrow in one's back for two years was a near impossibility, that an ordinary man would have died from the wound being infected. Bridger's reply, in typical Rocky Mountain fashion, was a growl accompanied with the words, *"Meat don't spoil in the Rockies."* It was one of Pa's best mountain man stories, one I would always remember. But at the moment that story had conjured up something else in my mind.

"You're the one who shot them Apache we were taking on earlier, weren't you?" I said as Shorty finished up his bandaging efforts. Things had been happening so fast out there that I couldn't be sure of what I saw, but I would have sworn it was Shorty handling that bow and arrow set of mine when those three Apaches had gone down.

"Y-e-a-h," he said, drawing the word out as though on purpose, although I wasn't sure at first just what that purpose was. But you can bet that know-it-all smile made me search my mind's eye further.

"Wait a minute," I finally said, feeling mighty suspicious all of a sudden. "Something ain't right."

"True." Damn it, he knew and he wasn't saying a damn thing about it! Worse, he was starting to get me mad. Then slowly it all came to me and I felt it all piece itself together in my mind as I spoke, the words forming in my brain just before they came out of my mouth.

"Them Apache went down awful fast," I said, which was a fact. They had indeed gone down quicker than a fighting bronco Apache would. Not that I'd had all that much to do with the Apache, you understand, but from my own experiences with the heathens who called themselves Indians, why, they were all pretty vicious when it came to fighting to stay alive. Hell, any man, no matter what the color of his skin, will do that. Besides, it ain't blood, like some will tell you, so much as the fear of dying that makes you fight like that.

"Like a fifty-pound sack of flour, that's a fact," he said, once again agreeing with me. I found myself wondering if his agreeability was supposed to be a hint that I had another clue to the puzzle in place.

"I take it then that you're a used-to-was mountain man of sorts, like Pa claimed to be. Knew Bridger and the rest?"

"That'd be right," Shorty said with a good deal of pride about him. The smile widened from ear to ear as he added, "Knew 'em all too, just like your daddy likely did."

"And I'd wager it was Bridger who taught you how to shoot a bow and arrow so good."

"Hell, no, boy!" he exclaimed with what sounded like outrage at first. "Why, ary Bridger saw me shoot the way I did earlier today, he'd have disowned knowing me, he would. That was some of the worse shooting I ever done in my lifetime."

"Couldn't be," I said with a frown, now feeling totally confused about what had happened. "The arrows stuck and them Apache went down and stayed down. No, that was damn good shooting."

"Well, ary it was, my friend, you helped me." Now he was chuckling, the only one who knew what in the hell was going on between us. It was getting on my nerves too.

"No. I couldn't have. Me and Wash and Emmett were out there taking on them Apache by our lonesomes when you shot the arrows."

"True, lad, but you're forgetting that they were *your* arrows." He slapped me on the back, making me flinch and grimace from the sore in my side, but he seemed to be having the laugh so why not.

"Oh, yeah," I said when the pain had settled down again and my mind was functioning the way it should. I had to pull back in my memory to piece it all together, but finally it all fit. This puzzle that Shorty Hall was throwing out to me in bits and pieces was finally making sense. Maybe he wouldn't be the only one to laugh at it after all.

He was right, they were my arrows. Any other time that wouldn't have mattered except that when I'd traded Quanah Parker for them, I'd had in mind killing those wolves who had been so much bother to us on the trail drive. You remember, the ones who had caused the stampede. And I'd gotten them too. That had been the start of it all.

"I'd bet a dollar to a pot of your coffee that I dipped every goddamn one of them arrows in that can of strychnine of yours," I said as a wave of relief came over me.

"So you saved your own life, didn't you?" Shorty said. "Worst shot that it was, all I had to do was nick them sonsabitches with an arrow and they was gone beaver."

"Yeah," I said, still wondering at the irony of the situation as I'd pieced it together. "I reckon you're right, Cookie."

Shorty took a long look around, as though to see if anyone else were in the area, then grabbed up his coffeepot, poured me a cup, and reached inside his chuck wagon. Once again taking a wayward gander about the area, he slipped out a jug of what could only have been home brew and added a couple of good swallows to my coffee.

"Seeing's you're just petrified as them forests Bridger says he found, I'll give you some of the Irish to calm you down," he said in a secretive way. "God knows you look like you need it."

It was the first hard liquor I'd had in a couple of months and it hit bottom like you'd expect. If it hadn't been mixed with a mite of coffee, why, I'd have had steam coming out of my ears and fire out of my nose. And I mean to tell you I didn't feel like one of them storybook dragons either.

"Thanks," I managed to grumble once I got my voice back. When I couldn't get anything else out, I indicated to Shorty I wanted more of the coffee to offset the kick of the Irish, or whatever it was he had poisoned the black stuff with. A warm-up and my voice soon returned to normal.

"Tell me something, Shorty," I said when I was through with the coffee.

"If I can." The man had resumed his cooking chores, apparently figuring his funning with me to be his easy time of the day.

"Just who did teach you to shoot a bow and arrow, if it wasn't Bridger?"

A smile of contentment came over him now. I knew he was reaching back into the past as he said, "Old Jim Beckwourth. Learned it when he was a Crow chief. Near killed old Liver-Eating Johnson oncet." He paused a moment in thought. Shaking his head, he added, "Nasty bunch of heathens when they wanted to be."

"I'll bet." I didn't doubt what the man was saying one bit, not one bit.

Yes, sir. I do believe Shorty Hall had more than one profession before he hooked up with Uncle Charlie Goodnight. But that's likely a whole 'nother canyon too.

CHAPTER

★ 16 ★

It wasn't until Cimarron was dead that I realized what a job Emmett had on his hands. I also got a real close look at how good Emmett had gotten with horses. Or maybe he had always been good and I'd never noticed it before. At any rate, Charlie Goodnight decided it would be a good idea for me to help out Emmett with the remuda, him being short a hand now and all. Not that Emmett was all that excited about having me to work with, you understand.

"What!" he yelled right in Charlie Goodnight's face when the boss told him the good news. I reckon he'd been with these mustangs long enough to figure he could say damn near anything he wanted to Uncle Charlie. "What do you think I am, some kind of chambermaid to the goddamn cook!" he roared, waving a hand off to somewhere or other just to be doing something. Emmett always had impressed me as being vocal with more than just his hands.

But Uncle Charlie, as the men had taken to calling Goodnight, wasn't taking to being scolded about anything, not today. With hands on hips, an authoritative eye cocked at Emmett, he replied, "Well, now, hoss, I reckon that can be arranged if it's to your liking."

"Hell, you might as well! All you've been giving me since this drive started is men and horses to break in, and I got to tell you, Goodnight, these cranky old mustangs are one hell of a lot easier to break in than the men you send me. A lot easier!"

By now I was sure the whole camp had heard Emmett and his complaining ways, for I doubted that the men who were showing up were here to listen in on the debate. No, sir. It was a fight they'd come to see, and whether they said so or not, I knew that in the back of their minds they wanted to see these two men tangle just as much as I did. Why, it had been a long time since any of us had seen a good foofaraw. A long time.

But not today. I had a notion Charlie Goodnight knew what they were gathering about for too when he turned to them and said, in one of his roughest growls, "What the hell are you pilgrims gawking at! Get back to that goddamn herd before they all take off and I send you back across the Llano to round 'em up." Any other time they might have fiddled around and taken their own good time getting back to the job, but Goodnight mentioning the possibility of them having to go back across the Llano Estacado to round up a bunch of mule-headed longhorns, why, that did the trick. It sure did. The crowd dispersed quicker than a lynch mob being talked to from the business end of a lawman's shotgun. I reckon seeing he still had the fire in him made Charlie Goodnight stoke up the flames a mite more as he turned to Emmett to read to him from the book.

"Emmett, you listen to me," he said, using that same growl he'd just used on the other men of the crew. "Carston here is gonna be working with you on this remuda, like it or not. Now, if you don't like it, why, you see me at the end of this drive and we'll fight over it, anyplace you want. But right now I've got more important things to do."

He stopped, turned to go, then stopped again and turned back to face Emmett. It wasn't settled yet, not by a long shot. "One other thing. You bellyache to me one more time about who I put to working with you and I'll assign Shorty Hall to work these horses and make you the cook!" Goodnight's arm shot out directly at Emmett, an action that sent a jolt of fear through him, of that I was sure.

"Jesus, Mary, and Joseph, don't do that!" the ex-sergeant said, a look of awe on his face, his eyes about to bulge out far enough to drop clean to the ground. Emmett had been around Wash and me long enough to know that if Wash and I had taken sick or gotten shot up, we'd likely have starved for Emmett can't cook worth a lick. It's one of the few things I'll admit I ain't too awful good at, either. Never have been. But give me a Colt and . . .

"You don't think I will, you just bellyache some more, wrangler," Goodnight said with a wink and a nod, addressing Emmett by his title rather than his name. Then he was gone and I knew that was that.

Not wanting to come in between Charlie Goodnight

and Emmett again, I decided to do my best with Emmett and the remuda.

There are some men who have a way with certain things in their lives that others couldn't touch if they wanted to. With me its damn near any kind of firearm I can get my hands on. With Emmett it was horses. I already knew that he could look the meanest mustang alive in the eye and sweet talk him into letting him get near enough to him to rub him down and toss a blanket on him and then kick him hard as he could in the gut. Hell, I'd seen that more than once the times he'd been working with me back on our ranch outside of Twin Rifles. It was almost as though he knew what the horses wanted to hear and said the right words to them no matter how ugly and mean they might be dispositioned. Of course, you had to be able to do that as a sergeant in the army too, so there was no denying Emmett had gotten a goodly amount of training in this aspect of horse handling during the war. Whatever it was, Emmett had what it took to be a top notch wrangler, which is what you call the man in charge of the horses just about any place on these plains.

"Just what is it they've got you doing that makes you want to gripe so much, Emmett?" I asked as we mounted up. "Mostly all I seen you do is ride around keeping the horses together."

"Boy, have you got a lot to learn," was his only reply. And was he right.

"All you seen me do is sitting in a saddle," he said as we moved the remuda out after the last of the herd had left the area. "But hell, most everyone in this outfit sits a-horse." Then, in a much lower voice, he added, "Wouldn't be surprised if a good many of 'em are sitting on their brains, either."

What he did was study these mustangs he had

gathered here, getting some kind of mental picture of each horse's characteristics and habits. "This job ain't just a matter of sitting in the shade and eating a can of peaches, you know," he said. Looking about at the expanse of flat land we were covering, he added, "Hell, you couldn't find shade nor peaches in this land."

Emmett explained that it was best to keep an eye on the remuda, especially if and when they got restless.

"You mean like that time we crossed the Pecos to the east side, the time Cimarron got killed," I said. The horses had been skittish all right, although with good reason, it turned out.

"Yeah," he nodded. "Kept you busy as a little dog in high oats, didn't it?"

"I'll say."

"Well, Chance, you make sure you stay busy with this remuda, you understand?"

"Why's that?"

Emmett looked about in a secretive manner. "It's like this, see? You got spare time, why, the boss man expects you to rustle up wood and water for the cook."

"No!" It didn't sound like one of the duties of a horse wrangler at all.

"Hell, yes," he said with an affirmative nod. "Why, old Goodnight expects you to help Cookie wash and dry the dishes too. And grind coffee for him!"

"No," I said in disbelief.

"Oh, yes. Now, I don't mind tossing a loop and snaking in a piece of deadwood once in a while, but I'll be damned if I'm gonna wash and dry dishes. Ain't done that since Mama still told me what to do, and that's a long time back, a long time back."

We headed the horses out away from the herd, making sure we kept them away from any sort of tree line that might be in the area. As flat as this land was, you could begin to see tree lines in the far distant horizon, although they were scant to say the least. Horses, Emmett said, saw shadows in the timbers and often got spooky because of it. I didn't have to be told more, knowing what he meant as I recalled our experiences with the wolves that had bothered the herd for a few days.

"Where's Wash?" I asked about midmorning, suddenly remembering that I hadn't seen my brother since before breaking camp.

Emmett chuckled. "I reckon you could say he's swapped his bed for a lantern," he said and went on to explain that Wash had decided to try his turn at nighthawking the remuda. At the moment, my brother was likely catching some shut-eye in Shorty's chuck wagon, although I couldn't see how there could be much more room in the wagon for a man, as much as I'd heard clatter around in the damn thing.

For me the biggest part of working the remuda came with having a man's mount ready for him. Each man in the crew had a string of horses, usually two or three. He'd ride one horse for most of the morning, then change him around noon when the herd was grazing. Then he'd saddle up his third horse for his turn at night guard. This gave each horse in the string enough time to recuperate for four or five hours of what was usually hard work, especially when the days got as hot as they did for us on this drive.

We made it to Shorty's location where night camp was being set up long before the herd reached it. I spotted Wash helping the cook set up camp, pulling out a few pieces of deadwood from underneath the chuck wagon to keep the fires going.

"Wait till the rest of the boys see you doing that," I

said with a grin. According to Wash, I can get on his nerves at times. Me, I never figured him for having the right kind of sense of humor at the right time. Which says something about the difference in the way we think, I reckon.

Wash only smiled back. "This'll be set up long before any of the crew or the herd makes it here," he said. He must have gotten some sleep during the day to feel this frolicsome. "Besides, I'm the one who did all the cooking in my bachelor days, if you recall."

"Oh, yeah," I said, trying to act as though it was a distant memory suddenly coming back to me. "Sarah Ann's got you helping out with the dishes now, has she?"

"It really ain't all that bad, Chance," he replied.

"You mean you *like* washing dishes?" I asked, using a tone of disbelief for the second time that day.

"Let me tell you something, Chance. Just between you and me, brother to brother," he said. He gave a quick glance about the area, as though to be talking to me on a subject he considered private and not wanting anyone else to hear his words.

"If you like," I said, although I wasn't sure what it was that he could tell me that was so secretive about marriage.

"Do you know how much fun Sarah Ann and me have doing the dishes while you've dragged your sorry ass out on the porch to sit around and listen to yourself fart all night?"

"I'll bite."

Wash had a thoughtful look about him for a moment before he said, "No. I don't think I'll tell you after all."

"Better stay out of the sun, Wash," I said, walking away from him, "I think it's getting to you."

What in the hell could he be talking about? What could a man possibly do with a woman when they were washing and drying dishes? I found myself wondering.

"Do you miss Chance as much as I miss Wash?" Sarah Ann asked Rachel Ferris.

It was Sunday evening and business being light at the Porter Cafe, Big John had decided to close early, telling Sarah Ann to leave early if she wished. She'd taken her father up on the offer, for it wasn't often that she got an evening off. In a way she thought it was her father's way of trying to make up to her for raising his voice to her last week. She'd been on the way out of town when Rachel Ferris, Margaret's daughter, had spotted her and waved to her from the veranda of the Ferris House. Sarah Ann had pulled up in front of the boardinghouse and accepted Rachel's offer of a glass of lemonade. The two young women—Rachel was all of five years older than Sarah Ann—had been best of friends for some years now. Neither one could remember the last time the two of them had argued. This wasn't unusual, for friendship between women was a prized commodity in a land with precious few women in it.

Both women had taken a fancy to the Carston boys as they'd grown up in Twin Rifles. Rachel had liked Chance even before he'd left for the war back in '61. Likewise, Sarah Ann had begun to set her cap for Wash just about the time he'd ridden off to join Terry's Rangers that same year. If absence makes the heart grow fonder, then the four years the Carstons were away at war had done wonders for the women who loved them, whether they realized it or not. Wash and Chance had both been back over a year now, but so far Sarah Ann had been the only one to have landed a husband. She'd been thinking about the wonderful life she and Wash had when it crossed her mind that Rachel hadn't said much about Chance of late. All of which brought up her question that evening on the veranda of the Ferris House.

"Oh, I miss him all right," Rachel said, Sarah Ann noticing a hint of hopelessness in her friend's voice. "I just wonder if he's missing me."

"Don't be silly, Rachel," Sarah Ann said in her best uplifting tone, "of course he does."

"I don't know, Sarah Ann." Once again there was doubt in Rachel's words. "Sometimes I don't think he knows I exist."

"He doesn't?" Sarah Ann found this hard to believe. Rachel was as beautiful a girl as she'd ever seen, and no one could ever fault her for her kindness, unless it was that she had too much of it. Sarah Ann simply frowned at Rachel with a confused face.

"I smile at him," Rachel continued. "I serve him the best cuts of meat at his meals when he's here. I speak kindly to him. Why, I even put up with his outrageousness." She let out a huge gasp of air that seemed to be all that her lungs could hold. Or maybe it was the pure exasperation that went with the expelling of that air that Sarah Ann noticed most. "But he doesn't seem to notice me at all. Not a whit." Her eyes drifted to the sky and the quickly disappearing sunlight of the day, as though the stars held the answers to her questions.

"Don't you worry, Rachel, he'll come around," Sarah Ann said. "I'll have Wash talk to him about it."

"Oh, no, don't do that." Rachel was suddenly in a panic. "Why, if Chance has to be *told* to give me a kiss, he'll be doing it because his brother told him to and for no other reason." A set look about her now, she added, "No, Sarah Ann, he's got to do it of his own will. His own accord."

"If that's the way you want it." Sarah Ann sipped her lemonade and took in the evening proper, acting as though the conversation were over and she was simply getting ready to leave to go home.

"He'll come around, won't he, Sarah Ann?" For being five years older, Rachel Ferris sounded as though she was looking to the older sister she never had for advice of the confidential nature. "He's got to know I love him. He's just got to."

The woman was about to break into tears, that much was evident to Sarah Ann, when a thought crossed her mind and an impish smile touched the corners of her mouth.

"Well, I don't suppose there's any harm in giving the man a little help," she said, the smile on her face broadening.

"A little help?" This time it was Rachel who had the confused look about her.

"Did I ever tell you what Wash and I do when we're washing and drying the dishes?" Sarah Ann said in a low voice. The sun had nearly gone down by now, so Rachel could barely make out the flushed look on her best friend's face as she spoke.

"No," she replied, still confused although very much interested. "No, you haven't."

"Well, it's about time I did." Sarah Ann gave Rachel's hand a firm confident squeeze. Then she proceeded to tell her best friend about those nights she and her husband washed the dishes, nights that she considered to be some of the most intimate of her married life thus far.

CHAPTER

★ 17 ★

Everything seemed to go a hell of a lot better after that last run-in with the Apaches who'd tried to steal our remuda and wound up killing Cimarron instead. The rattlesnakes were scarcer and scarcer, the water more plentiful as we headed north toward Fort Sumner and the New Mexican Territory. As for the Apaches, well, let's just say they were out there all right. They just weren't foolish enough to try pilfering what they knew was ours in the first place. But you can bet your bottom dollar they had an eye on us damn near every day of the rest of the drive, likely some nights too. They were doing a heap more of looking and seeing than they were fighting, I'll tell you that, hoss.

The way I figured it, we had upwards of a hundred and fifty miles to go on this last leg of what Charlie Goodnight was referring to as a six-hundred-mile stretch. And if my numbers were still any good, that meant we'd made it through the better part of three quarters of this trail drive just by being where we were.

"That oughtta count for something," I said one day when I mentioned the fact to One-Armed Bill Wilson.

"Not really," he said with a noncommittal shrug. I got the impression the man was a real cynical type, worse than me if that's at all possible. At least if you listened to Pa talk.

"And how's that?" I asked, curious.

"Knew a feller oncet," he said, letting a wad of spit fly out of his mouth as soon as the words had come out. If there'd been a tarantula where that gob of spit landed, I swear it would have died then and there, the gob was that big. "Spent the better part of a summer breaking horses, he did. Had more sores than a festered mule by the time the season was over. But he survived, he did. Yes, sir." One-Armed Bill let fly another gob of spit and was silent, taking in the horizon before him.

"So?"

The man gave me an unexpected look of surprise, as though I hadn't caught on to something when I should have. "Why, the damn fool went out that night and got blind drunk is what happened to him."

"What's so hellacious about that? Hell, I been that way my own self a couple of times."

"Not old Pockets," Wilson said, drawing back on memory from the look now on his face. He chuckled as he added, "Poor fool couldn't hold his liquor worth a damn."

"What happened to him?" I asked, sensing some kind of danger had stepped in the man's path.

One-Armed Wilson's chuckle turned into a smile as he looked at me and said, "Fell in the water trough out back of the barn, he did. Damn fool drown himself."

"Too bad. But what's your point?"

He let fly another of his continuous gobs of spit before glancing my way in a slow, deliberate manner. Then, cocking a baleful eye at me, he said, "This drive ain't over yet, Chance. Not by a long shot."

I reckon what he was getting at was the fact that even if we'd survived coming over four hundred miles we still had more than a hundred to go. And he was right, I reckon. Anything could happen on this last leg of the drive. As I watched One-Armed Bill riding off, I found myself liking the philosophizing of Cimarron more than this man. Cimarron had a good shorty answer to your question without beating around the bush. This fellow, why, he wanted to mix storytelling with question answering, and right now I didn't have time for it.

Of course, I also made a mental note to stay away from water troughs the next time I decided to drink from a bottle of the hard stuff.

We didn't follow the Pecos River directly, mostly staying a few miles away from it, although I was pretty sure the longhorns had the smell of it in their nostrils if they ever got thirsty. But the river ran parallel with the trail Charlie Goodnight was blazing up to Fort Sumner, so we had it within our reach whenever we wanted it.

If you ever hear a fellow on Cimarron's side of humanity refer to the word *bosque*, you can be sure of two things, hoss. The first is the language he's talking is Spanish—or Mexican, depending on what region you're in—and the word means "forest." Look to one of your sides if the man is palavering about the area you're in and you'll likely find a stand of trees somewhere in sight too. Maybe even a full-size forest too, although the more of this land I saw, the more I was convinced that most of the wooded land in this country was back east.

Anyway, that's what we started seeing more of the farther north we got. More wooded area and more Mexicans. But then I reckon I should have expected that. After all, this was their land. We just took it from them, same as we'd taken Texas from them, the same as the white man had taken nearly all of this country from the Indian tribes of one sort or another.

We'd trailed north across the Delaware and Black Rivers, above the Carlsbad country, then crossed back east to place the stream between us and the Mescalero Apaches who, according to Charlie, rendezvoused in the Guadalupe Mountains off to the west. Like I say, things got real tame then for a while as we passed Comanche Springs and the Bosque Grande, the Big Timbers if you like literal meanings. All the while we were getting closer to the Bosque Redondo and Fort Sumner, the desert becoming less and less obvious as trees and greenery began to fill up the area more and more.

"Can't say as I've ever been to Fort Sumner," Wash said one night around the camp fire. "Know anything about it, Charlie?"

Charlie smiled some. I'd noticed that his facial expression had gotten a whole lot more pleasant now that we were through the Llano Estacado. "I reckon it's a lot like you, Wash."

"Oh?" My brother almost had a streak of red creeping up his neck. He gets shy that way, you know.

"Yeah. It's young, ain't been around long, but it'll likely be around for some time to come." Wash looked real relieved at Charlie's words. "Ain't but three years ago that Sumner was established as a reservation for the Navajo and Mescalero Indians. Got some eight thousand of 'em, I hear. It's a shame," he added, finishing off his coffee.

"What's that?" I asked.

"Ain't a fit place for a reservation," Charlie continued. "Couldn't farm the soil for nothing. Fuel's scarce as hen's teeth. And provisions . . . well, to say they're inadequate wouldn't come anywhere close to being right."

"And that's where we come in?"

"Provisions. Right. That's what my contract's for, delivering beef for the government and its reservation Indians."

"Split it up, will they?" One-Armed Bill asked.

"I doubt it," Charlie replied, shaking his head. "Likely give it to the Navajo, from what I hear."

"Oh?"

Charlie tossed a thumb over his shoulder in the direction we'd just come from. "Way I got it figured, that was likely Mescaleros you boys tangled with back there," he said, referring to the ones who'd first tried killing me and then succeeded in killing Cimarron. "Seems their agent got driven off over some kind of claims he wasn't dealing proper with the cattle they were supposed to be getting." Charlie shrugged. "Up and left the reservation. Must figure they're better off on their own."

"Strange," Wash said. "I can't recall seeing any in the last fifty miles or so."

"Don't worry, brother, they're out there," I said, speaking what I was sure Charlie and the rest of us already knew.

"Probably right." Wash set his tin cup down on Shorty's fold-down surface of the chuck wagon.

"Wash?"

My brother turned to face me before he left for his remuda.

"I wouldn't stop looking over my shoulder until I had four solid walls around me," I said in dead seriousness.

Wash nodded. "I understand."

CHAPTER

★ 18 ★

Wash didn't stop looking over his shoulder until we reached the outskirts of Fort Sumner. But he wasn't nothing special that way; hell, the rest of us were doing the same thing. I've got to admit though, it sure did feel a mite easier on my mind to see friendly faces looking our way for a change. Let me tell you, hoss, most of them Indians we'd tangled with were downright ugly in more ways than one. But at Fort Sumner, why, even the ugly folks looked right appealing.

The Bosque Redondo was a circular grove of giant cottonwood trees outside of Fort Sumner that now served as the reservation for the Navajo Indians Charlie had mentioned. But the idea for its use wasn't anything new. James H. Carleton, now a general in the

Union army, had originally recommended that the area be made into a cavalry post back in the 1850s, but his idea was largely ignored. It wasn't until he'd enlisted the aid of Kit Carson during the War Between the States to round up the Apaches and Navajos that the Bosque was put to good use as a reservation upon the capture of these tribes. Only then was Fort Sumner created for the stationing of military troops to guard the reservation Indians when they were placed on this largely unfarmable land. It didn't take but one long look at the land surrounding the Bosque Redondo to realize what might have driven the Indians from their reservation.

"Looks like company, Charlie," I said, pointing out three men who rode our way. We'd found some passable grazing for the longhorns and had just finished bedding them down about noon of that day. In a way, it surprised me that it took these fellows that long to spot our presence. Or maybe they were cattlemen too and had the good courtesy to let us get our work done first before they come a-calling. Men in the same profession will do that, you know.

"Would you be Goodnight?" the center man asked when he reined in his mount. He was all business from the look of him, a trimmed mustache and fancy broadcloth suit over a clean white shirt and string tie. I'd gauge he didn't have a speck of dust on him until he reached our herd of longhorns. No, sir. He looked mighty pretty compared to us, which was maybe the reason he frowned as he gave us the once over, looking down his nose as he did. I didn't like him and neither did Charlie and it showed.

"What the hell's it to you, pilgrim?" Charlie growled in his meanest trail drive voice, and I mean it was mean. The fellow's riding partners near had their heads shot back from Charlie's words. Me, I was laughing inside and trying not to show it.

"I'm Mr. Roberts," the man said, "the general contract—"

"That's your problem, son, not mine. Can't help what your name is or why your mama and daddy give you such a godawful one, no sir," Charlie said, still talking mean.

This Roberts fellow had patience, I'll give him that. "If you'll please let me finish," he said. "I'm the general contractor you'll be dealing with for the sale of your beef. These men are my subcontractors, Jim and Tom Patterson," he added, indicating the two riders with him who were also dressed in what I always thought to be a man's Sunday best. Who knew, maybe it was Sunday. I damn sure couldn't tell.

If Roberts was waiting for Charlie Goodnight to apologize for the way he'd spoken, I knew he'd still be sitting on that horse of his when the fires of hell went out.

"I heard you fellows was paying out upwards of sixteen cents a pound for meat on the hoof," Charlie now said in a more pleasant voice as he cocked a curious eye toward Roberts and his cohorts.

"You've been awful misinformed then, mister," Roberts said, half shaking his head in defiance. "At the most I'm authorized to pay you eight cents a pound on the hoof, and that's for your twos and threes and up. The cows and calves you've got in this herd I can't use at all." He paused a moment before adding, "Me and the Pattersons will cut out those steers we think we can use and we'll talk from there."

Without another word the three of them set about

going through our herd of longhorns, cutting out the stock they thought worth purchasing and leaving the cows and calves behind for us to do what we might with. At the end of the afternoon they had cut all but eight hundred of our original herd for purchase. Roberts and Charlie did some dickering then and came out with just over twelve thousand dollars in cold hard cash as the sale price for all but those eight hundred head of cows and calves. For Charlie Goodnight and Oliver Loving—and all the rest of us, I reckon—it was a small fortune.

Shorty accompanied Charlie into Fort Sumner the next day and picked up some supplies while Charlie got his $12,000 in payment for the herd. When they returned we made our way up the Pecos to a creek called Las Carretas where we set up camp near some decent water and grass for our horses.

"Now before you boys go wandering off, they had some mail for some of you back at Fort Sumner," Shorty said when we all grouped around the chuck wagon.

"Well, don't just stand there, give it out!" Emmett yelled. A chorus of agreement went up and Shorty produced a half dozen letters and began reading names off.

"Carston!" he said in a loud voice after four of the letters had been handed out to various men in the crew.

"Here," I said and began to reach for the letter, although I couldn't imagine who would be writing me.

"Not you," the cook said. "They likely figure you can't read anyway." He looked past me and spotted my brother. "Here, Wash, this one's for you."

"Thanks," my brother said in a grateful tone and set

about opening and reading his mail. I knew it had to be from Sarah Ann.

"Halliday," Shorty called out, reading off the name on his last piece of mail, but nobody answered his call. "Halliday? Ain't nobody here go by the moniker of Halliday?"

"Say, Shorty," I heard Charlie say in a low voice to his cook.

"Yeah, boss."

"Didn't you tell me one time that was your name?"

Shorty Hall was silent for a brief moment, going over Charlie's words in his mind. He wouldn't have been the first man to have shortened his name or changed it somehow when arriving in a new part of the country. Suddenly, it hit him. "Oh. Yeah. I reckon you're right," he said and shoved the letter in his pants pocket.

"Halliday, huh?" I said, a grin on my face. Hell, someone had to give him a hard time.

"Don't even ask, Chance. Don't even ask," Shorty Hall, or Halliday, said.

Wash had a satisfied smile about him as he read his letter from Sarah Ann.

"All that mush about loving you and all, is that it?" I asked him when he was halfway through the letter.

"Yeah," he smiled, a bit of red creeping up his neck. "Now shut up and let me finish this." I did as he requested and stood there a couple more minutes, but by the time he was finished, Wash didn't have a pleasant look on his face at all. Not at all.

"What's the matter?" I asked. "Everyone's all right, ain't they?"

"Yeah. It's just that Sarah Ann had a visit from some tough-looking stranger who said he was looking for you. If Pa hadn't been there, she doesn't know what this fella would've done. Seems Pa told him to get out and leave her alone." As Wash relayed the contents of the letter, I noticed him become more and more worried. It almost seemed as bad as when we'd first started out on the drive.

"Don't worry, brother," I said, placing a firm hand on his shoulder, "she'll be all right. I told you Pa and the others would look after her."

But that didn't seem to do much good and I followed Wash over to where Charlie Goodnight was having a cup of coffee, not sure what he had in mind.

"You got any objections if I leave, now that the drive is over, Charlie?" he asked the boss.

"Of course not. When did you want your pay?"

"Tomorrow morning would be fine," Wash said, urgency now in his voice. "I think there's trouble back home."

"Well, I'm sorry to hear that, Wash," Charlie said. He set his cup down. "But I'll tell you what, if you can wait an hour or two after daylight, I'll go back with you."

"Strength in numbers?" I asked.

"Among other things. Oliver Loving and me talked it over just now and he'll be taking those remaining eight hundred head up toward Colorado. One-Armed Bill Wilson is going with him. Me, I'm heading back to Fort Belknap and see can I round up another herd to bring out here before the snow flies. Just a suggestion."

"Sounds good to me," I said, hoping I was speaking for both my brother and me.

"Then it's done," was all Charlie said before wandering off to something else.

"You're gonna have to stop worrying, Wash," I said

when we were alone. "Like I said, she's being taken good care of."

"Chance, did it ever cross your mind that no matter how many friends she's got, they can't all be with her at the same time?"

I couldn't think of anything to say.

She had the eeriest feeling as she left the barn for the ranch house. It was that strange sort of feeling you got when you thought someone else was watching you but you couldn't be sure. Dallas Bodeen had accompanied her home that night. He'd even helped her put up the horses before leaving. He had wanted to stay longer but she had assured him everything was all right, that all she had to do now was clean up and go to bed. After all, it was almost sundown. It had been a long day for Sarah Ann at the Porter Cafe and she wanted nothing more now than to climb into bed and sleep.

Suddenly she knew someone was indeed behind her and, standing before the front door, she froze in place. She wheeled around, hearing the faintest of noises behind her, and let out a gasp of fear.

He was there! Standing by the hitching rail was the stranger, the one who had originally confronted her when Will Carston had joined her for supper that day two weeks ago. But Will wasn't here to protect her. Nor was Dallas, who she had shooed on home to the Ferris House in Twin Rifles. That meant she was alone with this man and, in truth, it scared her something fierce.

"Omigod," she said, letting out the only words that would come to her as she recognized the man now before her.

"Howdy, ma'am," he said with what looked like the same leer she'd seen on his face last time. He took too much pleasure in speaking his words and, like last time, she didn't like it. Not one bit.

"What do you want?" If the words sounded like they came from a frightened woman, it was because that was exactly how she felt.

"I could say I come for you." In the full moon she could see the leer grow even wider as the stranger took a step toward her.

"That would be a big mistake, mister, not to mention the last one you ever made." When the stranger turned to his rear he saw Dallas Bodeen standing not far from him, a Henry rifle cradled across the crook of his arm, the barrel pointed right at the stranger's midsection.

"Thank God you're here, Dallas," Sarah Ann said with a sigh of relief.

"Where'd you come from, old man?" the stranger asked Dallas. "I thought you'd left?"

"Oh, I started to, all right, I started to," Dallas said, a grin crossing his own face now, the kind you'd find on any fox when he's cornered his prey. "It was that whiff of tobacco I smelled on the way out that give me second thoughts. I knew Sarah Ann hadn't taken to rolling her own, so I snuck on back. Now suppose you tell me what it is you want here."

"Nothing," the stranger said, apparently realizing that the man with the rifle was no match against his holstered six-gun. "Like you say, it was a mistake. I reckon I'll be riding on."

"You do that," Dallas said as the stranger mounted up. "And mister?"

"Yeah?"

"I never had second thoughts about killing a rattlesnake. I see you around here again, I'll shoot first and bury you where you fall."

The stranger didn't have to see Dallas Bodeen's face to know that the man was dead serious in what he said.

Only when the rider had disappeared into the night did Sarah Ann rush into the safety of Dallas Bodeen's arms.

The One-Mile Waltz

CHAPTER
★ 19 ★

Men like Shorty Hall are hard to change. I say that because the trail drive might have been over for the most part, but he was still set in his ways, so to speak, and was ready with breakfast at first light the next morning. The contractor and his men had parted with the portion of the herd he'd purchased, leaving only the eight hundred head of stock Oliver Loving would soon be trailing up toward Colorado. Maybe that was why Shorty had our food ready for us that early. I don't know. What I did know was that Wash was up and ready to move then and there while I was still rolling out of the blankets. It was a wonder he opted to stay for a morning meal.

"Say, what's this I hear about you boys heading back to Texas?" Emmett asked as he poured himself another cup of coffee. "Is that for sure, or is that just Cookie here flapping his lips and trying to make useless gossip again?" I noticed that the big man's words came out only half in jest, mostly, I was sure, because he too had a woman back in Twin Rifles.

"It's no rumor, hoss," Charlie said. "We'll be heading out soon's we finish up Cookie's coffee here."

Emmett was thoughtful a moment, although I thought I knew what he was pondering about. "Got room for another rider?" he finally asked, cocking a curious eye toward the three of us.

"What about—" Charlie started to say, but Emmett beat him to it.

"I got Lance broke in good enough to handle these gentles," he said, tossing his thumb over his shoulder at the remuda that still stood intact. Looking at those horses it crossed my mind that we'd come through the drive pretty well when you considered man flesh and horse flesh. Except for Cimarron and two of the horses, all of us had made it through in one piece, although there were times . . .

"He's right, Charlie," Wash said with a nod. "That young lad's turning out to be right handy with the remuda." Lance had been a youngster who was willing to take a crack at picking up where Cimarron had left off with the horse herd and had done quite well for himself. A real no-nonsense type, he was.

Charlie Goodnight was rubbing his jaw in a thoughtful manner his own self.

"Well, he is, you know," Emmett said, almost on the verge of sounding desperate.

"Oh, I know he is," the boss man replied. "I was just running some figures through what's left of my mind." A few more moments of silence and he added, "How's twelve hundred sound to you fellas?"

"Huh?" all three of us said in unison, not knowing what in the devil he was talking about.

"You know, for the herd."

I gulped hard, suddenly realizing what he was talking about. "The herd? You mean *dollars?*"

"You was planning on selling those mustangs to me, wasn't you?" he asked in near astonishment.

I'd clean forgot about the money angle of this whole adventure we were on, at least until he'd mentioned buying the herd from us.

Emmett smiled for the first time that day. "The memory of all those blisters we worked up is growing a mite easier on me now," he said. We'd all three, Emmett, Wash, and me, agreed that we'd divvy up the money three ways and I could just see the ex-sergeant working the figures in his mind now.

"Give it up, Emmett," I said with what I'm sure was a leer as I took in both Emmett and my brother, who had that same sort of grin growing about him now. "Your women have already got that money spent."

"He's probably right," Shorty said as though he were a knowing man on the subject.

"Which is why I'm still single," I added with a leer.

Charlie Goodnight had packed a mule with enough provisions to make it across the dreaded Llano Estacado, along with the twelve thousand dollars in gold he'd gotten for the sale of the herd. All of us knew too well that there wasn't a lick's worth of habitation on that godforsaken stretch of so-called land, not a lick's worth. So if we looked as though we were loaded up for a winter's worth of trapping in the Rockies, well, we likely were. We were just headed in another direction.

Along with our fastest horse, each of us rode a

saddle mule when we set out on our back trail. Naturally, we rode the mules more for their staying qualities than anything else. After all this wasn't no parade we were taking off on. And, hoss, I can guarantee you that in a land like the Llano Estacado, staying quality is all that counts, for looking pretty ain't worth a damn out there. Besides, in case of an Indian attack our plan was to mount those fast horses and abandon our mules while we shot our way out if that was what was necessary. And with Indians you never could tell.

I knew all too well we were headed back into Apache and Comanche country. I reckon the scariest thought about that was that Quanah Parker had claimed he'd give me safe passage across the Llano Estacado. But he hadn't said a damn thing about coming back and just the thought of that could make a man skittish.

We rode all that day, then down the Pecos at night, laying up in out-of-the-way places the following day. The heat had been rough so we waited until evening and as dusk fell took to the trail again. There is a rule you learn if you plan to go much farther than your hometown out here. It says, *"Always watch your back trail, for things look different when you're going in the opposite direction."* Charlie Goodnight had gotten right good at that, for he led us down the Pecos all the way, never missing a twist or a turn in that snaky river.

"Better break out the slickers, boys," Charlie said when he pulled to a halt and took in the massive amount of dark clouds off in the distance.

"Won't argue with you a bit, boss," Emmett said as he dug out his slicker. "War clouds gathering, I see."

"More ways than one," I said and gave a look

toward the southwest, where the Guadalupe Mountains jutted out the nearest to us that I recalled seeing. "You ask me, we'd hit the most dangerous part of this trail."

"Know what you mean, brother," Wash said in agreement. He knew that the closer we got to those mountains, the supposed rendezvous of the Mescaleros, the closer we were to likely getting an arrow in our ribs.

"Don't think on it too much, boys, or you'll never make it back to your sweethearts," was all Charlie had to say on the subject before moving out again.

It was a storm heading our way all right and it struck just as hard as it looked. There was lightning, thunder, and rain and a lot of heavy winds, but we pushed on. We had to.

It was at the worst part of the storm that all hell broke loose.

Something scared the pack animal. I never could tell whether it was the weather itself or some of those damned Apaches. Whatever it was, that mule took off like a bat out of hell. I reckon the four of us were thinking more of the money on that mule than any provisions it might have been carrying, for we all took off on those mules, spurring the hell out of them and pushing them to their limit as we chased that mule for a good quarter mile. I don't know whether Charlie Goodnight was greedier than the rest of us or just a mite more crazy, but when he got up next to that running mule, why, he flung himself off his own mount and grabbed that damned runaway as he went by. Could have killed himself doing it too. Hell, you have to remember that we'd been traveling at night now, so all we had to see by was the lightning flashes for there sure wasn't any full moon out. And I know that even if there was, we wouldn't have been able to see by it worth a damn. All I can say is Charlie got almighty lucky for he managed to grab the pack rope, which was tied to the animal's neck. But that didn't stop the mule, for he was bucking and running and bellowing like he was born to and still trying to get away. It was Wash and me who managed to get out in front of that mule and bring him to a final stop.

"Looks like you worried him to a standstill, Uncle Charlie," Wash said with a grin.

"You all right, Charlie?" I asked.

"Yeah, I'm all right," he said in a relative soft voice compared to the loudness he could reach. Then a smile came to him as he added, "You know, between the two of us I reckon that mule and me tore up enough ground for a circus."

"We still got the money?" a worried Emmett said, riding up with Charlie's horse in tow.

"I knew a wrangler would come in handy on this trip," Charlie said as he took the reins of the horse.

"But have we still got the money?" Emmett was sounding more and more desperate about the money situation.

Charlie went to checking the provisions on the mule and came up shaking his head.

"Oh, hell," Emmett said in that worried voice he was using more and more. "It's gone, ain't it? The money's gone." I knew from the expression on his face that he was watching his small fortune dashed in a few short minutes of a rainstorm.

"Oh, the money's here, Emmett, you won't have to

worry about that," Charlie said, relieving Emmett's worry for a few moments.

"Then what is it, Charlie?" This time it was Wash who was showing concern.

"It's the goddamn provisions. They're gone."

Now we were really in a fix!

CHAPTER

★ 20 ★

We looked around the area, searching for the lost supplies, but it wasn't much use. Not a trace of them was anywhere near at hand that we could see. And you couldn't see a hell of a lot in that darkness, even after the storm let up. All that was left to do was make camp where we now stood. I don't mind telling you that I did it in a right hesitant manner too, for I hadn't forgotten that this was the most dangerous spot to be on this road. And I'm not talking thunder-boomers.

What sleep we got was fitful at best. When daylight came we were hoping we'd have better luck at finding some of those provisions, but such wasn't the case. Not in our area, anyway.

"Would you look at that?" Emmett said, holding up what looked like a piece of bacon maybe six inches square and nowhere close to thick. "A goddamn piece of fatback."

"Don't cuss it too much, hoss," Charlie said with a straight face, "it might be the only thing we find of those provisions."

Emmett made a big deal out of dusting the sand and mud off the bacon before stuffing it in his pocket, shaking his head in disgust as he did.

We spread out from the area where we'd made night camp, each of us going in one direction, agreeing to search that general area for any sign of the provisions. If and when we found something, we also agreed to fire one shot into the air for the others to come to us. No one had to ask to know that if they heard more than one shot, he'd better converge on the other and do it with guns drawn, for there would likely be Indian trouble to contend with.

I was off to the east when I heard a shot come from Charlie Goodnight's direction. Reflexes had my hand on my Colt, waiting for a second shot to be fired, but by the time I'd wheeled my mount around in his direction, I knew the one shot was all that had been fired. In a way it made me feel a mite easier, for I'd much rather find some well-needed food than fight a bunch of battle hungry Apaches.

But Charlie was just shaking his head, much like Emmett had done not long ago, when the three of us pulled our mounts to a halt by our boss man.

"Look at that, will you?" he said, pointing to what appeared to be numerous tracks. I squinted a mite and saw that they were coyote tracks, a lot of coyote tracks. "Bastards must've got all of it. Even took my goddamn tobacco." It looked like the coyotes had indeed carried away the sacks of makings Charlie had packed for himself.

"Don't leave us much in the line of food, does it?" Wash said.

"Not if you count that piece of bacon Emmett's got," Charlie said. "If he ain't et it yet."

"Not hardly," was Emmett's stern reply as he pulled the bacon from his pocket.

"I reckon we could always hunt up them coyotes," I said, trying to make light of the situation. "Eat all that food of ours, why, they ought to be right fat and sassy."

"Shut up, Chance," Wash said.

So much for displaying a sense of humor about then.

We holed up the rest of the day and started our trek again come nightfall. The sky had cleared up and there was indeed a bit of a moon out for us to see at some of the country we were riding through.

The bacon had been rinsed off with river water and cut into four equal pieces during the afternoon, each of us savoring the small amount of food we had left. But I don't think any of us were really all that worried, for we had water if nothing else. You see, hoss, when it comes right down to it, why, food ain't much more than a luxury for most folks. Oh, we get to eating it on a regular basis and grow old getting fat and cheeky, but when it comes right down to it, food ain't nothing more than a pleasure. A body can go a long while without food if he has to, and more than one man can attest to that fact. What you need to keep alive just about anywhere in this world is *water*. Ain't no two ways about it. And the truth of the matter was we had the whole Pecos River to swallow up if we had it in our disposition to. Of course, after seeing the gluttons those longhorns had made of themselves once we'd gotten across the Llano Estacado, why, I had no such intention whatsoever. But it was a mite comforting to know that that much water was only a short ways off.

Feeling comfortable, on the other hand, didn't last too long.

"Look out, Charlie, there's a rattler!" I heard Wash yell.

"What? Huh?" It took Charlie more than a short moment to notice what my brother was pointing out to him. Once he did, he managed to guide his horse out of the way of the rattlesnake off to his side.

I gave Emmett and Wash a silent look, wondering if they knew what was going on, for usually Charlie Goodnight was an observant man. At the moment, though, he was anything but that. All Emmett and Wash could do was shrug at my tacit concern.

Not fifteen minutes went by before I spotted another rattler. Charlie didn't.

"Damn it, Charlie, there's another rattler," I said in my own booming voice. A fleeting question crossed my mind as I wondered if we were getting back into that part of the Pecos where old Cross-Eye had such fun hunting up those snakes. By the time Charlie had his horse out of the way, and he did so just barely, I pulled out my Colt and shot the snake's head off.

"Sonofabitch," I murmured as I reholstered the six-gun. "Wait a minute, people, just wait a minute," I then added, reining in my mount. "Charlie, just what the hell's going on?" If he saw I was mad, he didn't seem to care. Well, neither did I. Hell, I wasn't about to spend my whole rest of the trail time back to Fort Belknap shooting rattlers that Charlie Goodnight couldn't take care of his own self. Not by a long shot.

We took a break then and Charlie explained that when he had been in the rangers years ago, he had one hellacious bout with the measles. I had heard they could be death on grown men. Some of Charlie's senses hadn't returned to their full strength, particularly his hearing. It seems that when he got terrible sick or had himself a bad cold, why, his hearing went all to hell, as though his ears were purely blocked up.

"I reckon this drive has taken more out of me than I figured it would," he finally admitted, reasoning that this was the reason his hearing hadn't picked up the rattles on those snakes. We all knew that having keen senses was a critical factor in staying alive in this land and knew what Charlie must be feeling. Charlie, on the other hand, wasn't interested in any social understanding or pity today. A frown came to his forehead as he said, "You boys better stop yelling at me like some damn fool."

"But Charlie, all we was trying to do was warn you for your own good," Wash said. I reckon that sounded too reasonable to Charlie.

"Well, you can take your damned rattlers and go straight to hell or any other place you want to, and leave me alone," he growled at my brother and jerked his reins to leave, heading down the Pecos again.

"Well, now," Emmett said, watching the stubborn Texan go, "ary the man wants to act that way, I'll just let the goddamn rattlers bite him next time they're about." His words had that I'll-show-you air about them, if you know what I mean.

"Likely wouldn't do any good, hoss," I said, slowly reining my own horse to follow Charlie.

"How's that?"

"One thing I've noticed about Charlie Goodnight, Emmett, is that he gets streaks of piss ugly mean in him," I said. "Like now."

"And?"

"Hell, a rattler bit him the mood he's in now, why,

the snake would likely die," I said with a straight face. "The shock would kill off all that snake's young 'uns too."

"I reckon that's just as well," Wash said, pulling up beside us.

I took in his words and began wondering at their meaning. "Oh?"

"Maybe it hasn't crossed your minds, fellas, but if we don't come across some kind of food in the not too distant future, why, those rattlers will be the only food left for us on the face of this earth," my brother said, half smiling.

"Not hardly," Emmett said in his adamant fashion.

"Ain't that the truth," I added. "Why, I'll eat that goddamn mule first before I settle for one of them vipers on my plate!"

"I don't think Charlie will like that."

"Don't care what he likes," I said, adding my own bit of steadfastness to my voice. "That goddamn animal's responsible for us going without now. Seems to me he ought to be able to give his all—and I do mean *all*—when it comes down to the last."

For the first time in a long time, I thought my brother's smile was indicative of the man actually enjoying something. It was the first time in a long time I'd seen him smile like that.

"Charlie ain't gonna like it," he said.

"Hell, the mule ain't gonna like it," I replied, "but at this point I ain't taking no back talk from him neither."

CHAPTER

★ 21 ★

It wasn't that we had to have food, you understand. Like I said, as long as we had water, we could survive this land. Maybe it was the fact that our stomachs started to growl so loud, even in the dark. Or should I say especially in the dark? We had no provisions and knew all too well there wouldn't be any game, so to speak, for the next two hundred miles, so about sunup we stopped at the Pecos and shot a couple of catfish for breakfast.

"You sure that's wise?" Charlie asked once Wash and me were through shooting the catfish.

"Hell, Charlie, if the damned Apaches don't hear those shots, they'd likely be hearing our stomachs, as loud as the bunch of us are," Emmett said, cocking a rueful eye at Goodnight. "Besides, we ate the bacon, rind and all, and you know good and well that wasn't about to last us back to Belknap. So stop asking stupid questions."

"I'll tell you what, boys," I said to both of them, hoping I could keep a fight from taking place. Not that I'm against a good fistfight, you understand. Hell, no. It was just that this wasn't the time or the place for any of us to be doing something as foolish as that. As Pa would put it, I tried to be the cooler head that prevailed. "You want to open up a discussion, why, you ask Wash what he thinks about the last book he's read. I understand that Dickens fella has put out some fine reading. As for me, I'm gonna cook me some breakfast," I added with a smile and held up the two catfish on my makeshift string.

I reckon my words got across to Charlie and Emmett with all the intent I had meant them to, for they settled down and did nothing more than ignore one another while we ate our catfish breakfast, or supper, or whatever the hell meal you wanted to call it.

Whatever meal of the day it was, it sure did add some strength to the four of us. We filled our canteens and agreed that it was time to travel during the day as well now, for it was time to cross the Pecos and strike our luck at making it back across the Llano Estacado.

"Wasn't no Injuns on the way across it, ary I recall," Charlie said. "Don't guess there oughtta be any going back across the damn thing."

"True," Emmett said in agreement. I didn't think these two would ever speak to one another again, but I reckon that's what happens when your belly gets filled after being empty the better part of a day and some. "Those heathens got more sense than to be out in this type of weather. Not like us crazies."

"Besides, ain't no place to hide on the Llano," Wash said.

"For them or us," I said, throwing in one extra line of thought in case no one had conjured it up yet. If all you're doing is standing there and trying to kill one another outright and doing it face to face, why, your chance is as good as your opponent's, if you ask me.

I don't know about the rest, but about noon that day I was thinking we should have found us some shade for the day and kept our marching to the nighttime. It was hotter than the devil, hotter than I thought I remembered it being when the dust and heat and shale and dirty smell all ricocheted back on us from that herd of longhorns not long ago. It didn't seem like anything had changed, nothing at all. The only thing missing now was the longhorns, for all the rest of the elements were there. And I don't mind telling you, hoss, that by noon it was taking its toll on me. I'd finished a half a canteen, an amount of water that should have lasted me for at least a day under these circumstances. I could say that I couldn't help myself, but it would be an out-and-out lie. I made myself a promise then and there. But I made it to Wash, just so it would mean something to me. You know how it is, you make a thousand promises to yourself and then tell yourself "not this time" later on. But when you make a promise to a man, why, you've got to keep it.

"Wash, do me a favor, will you?" I said about midafternoon, my mouth full of dust and the taste of shale.

"If I can."

"From here on out, no matter how broke we get, don't ever let me talk us into doing something this crazy again."

"You mean rounding up a bunch of wild mustangs

and breaking them and coming on a trail drive with the likes of Charlie Goodnight?" he said with what I took to be a smile forming on his face.

"No, not the rounding up mustangs and breaking them. Maybe not even going on a godforsaken trail drive."

"Then what exactly have you got in mind, Chance?"

I looked him straight in the eye and, with a dead serious look, said, "Don't ever let me be fool enough to try making this trek across the Llano Estacado."

"Know just what you mean. Same goes here." Wash stuck his hand out and we shook on it, sealing the bond if ever one needed it.

On we went, pushing ourselves through that furnace called a desert, once again looking like highwaymen as the wind picked up and we pulled our bandannas up over our mouths and noses. And on we did go. We had to. It was useless as buffalo chips in one of those fancy back east salads to turn back, crazy in fact. It was just as useless to stop for we'd fry under the burning heat of the merciless sun. So we went on, praying to ourselves, I was sure, that our horses would make it through the day even if we didn't. Only once did I let the thought cross my mind as to how bad off I'd be trying to cross this wasteland on foot. Believe me, son, if they ever tell you that a man without a horse is nothing, you take real good stock in that, for that man knows what he's talking about.

I kept looking to my front, wanting in the worst way to see the Concho River before me, the last big watering hole we'd left before making our way across the Llano with our herd of longhorns. It was late that afternoon that Charlie pulled to a halt and I thought we had reached it. After all of this riding through hell, we'd reached the Concho!

But we hadn't.

"Now, what the devil is that?" was all Charlie said as he peered off in the distance. I had to squint more than once to clear my eyes to see what he was taking in. Whatever it was, it was a mass of black off in the distance, off on the horizon. But it was still in the desert with no river in sight.

"Indians?" I said, saying the first thing that came to my mind.

"Could be."

"But there ain't supposed to be none of them out here," Emmett said, squinting at the mass just as hard as I had.

"Maybe twenty of 'em," Charlie said, at the same time taking out his six-gun and checking the loads. The rest of us were soon doing the same thing.

Suddenly I felt a chill run up my spine. At any other time I would have welcomed it, especially in this heat. But at the moment it only spelled fear to me and I felt a premonition of doom pass over me with it. I looked at the others, wondering if they felt the same way. I knew Charlie did by the words he spoke.

"Strange, ain't it," he said. "Here we are with more gold than any of us has likely seen in all his life, and it won't buy you a drink of water or a plate full of food. And if them are Apache, we may be dying for something as useless as gold."

"Know what you mean," I said. A man spends the better part of his life trying to make a dollar to save, usually wanting gold and money and all the fixings so bad he can taste it. But when he gets this close to death and dying, why, ain't none of it seems worth a damn.

All I knew was that the only thing worth much at all to me right then and there was my hide, worthless as it might seem to most of the rest of the world.

"Ask me, it's time to quit these mules and mount up our horses again," Emmett said.

"Wouldn't argue it one bit," Wash said, and we were soon off our mules and mounted on our horses. And I'll tell you, friend, even facing the odds we were against those Indians, if that's what they were, I for one felt one whole lot easier about it on my horse. After all, there's just so much dragging your feet on the ground a man can take, especially riding a god-damn mule.

"You boys keep hold of them mules and your horses," Charlie said. "I'll open up a lane through them Injuns with my pistols."

"You mean *we'll* open up a lane through them Injuns," I said, digging inside my saddlebags and pulling out a second holster and Colt army model .44. I was fitting it through the left side of my belt when I said, "You ain't the only one who's served in the Texas Rangers, you know."

I handed the reins of my mule to Emmett, who only frowned and gave me a harsh look of contempt. "Would you look at that," he said, shaking his head in disbelief. "A cavalryman stuck with goddamn mules."

There was no use hurrying death, so we walked our horses toward the black mass in the distance. Slowly, it got bigger and bigger, but it didn't seem to spread out as I'd seen most war parties do.

"Maybe it ain't Injuns," Charlie said.

"We'll find out soon enough." Conversation was drying up real quick, almost as fast as the inside of my mouth.

The mass kept growing and growing as it moved toward us, but I was soon betting that we'd make it through the day without losing our hair. In fact, it looked more and more like a wagon with a hell of a big load on it. Turns out that's just what it was, a six-yoke ox team and a wagonload of the biggest watermelons I do believe I ever saw!

The driver was a man named Rich Coffee. He hailed from the upper settlements on the Colorado, just below the mouth of the Concho. I got the impression Charlie Goodnight and this fellow had a passing acquaintance with one another, so I let them do all the palavering.

"Where you headed, Rich? Wrong time of the year to be meeting caravans, ain't it?" Charlie said. If he felt a mite more easy about the Indians who didn't turn out to be Indians after all, well, so did I.

"Heading for the Pecos," Rich Coffee said, "over to the great Salt Lake to load back with salt." He seemed like an easygoing enough man, but then you never could tell. Most of the men I'd met the last couple of months had seemed easygoing to begin with and turned out to be something else all together. "Sell these watermelons to the Mexicans. Come there from the El Paso country twicet a year, you know."

"Well, Rich, you got customers right here if you're willing to part with a couple of them melons," Charlie said. It's a good thing he said it too, for if he didn't I would have.

Like I said, it was late afternoon, so we didn't have any trouble finding shade on the far side of his wagon as we sat there and each had a cool watermelon or two. The man was kind enough to stop there for a couple of hours before leaving on his way.

By the time he'd left he gave us enough provisions to make it to Fort Belknap. And we did that without much trouble until the very last.

But I'll tell you, hoss, next to that godawful heat, I reckon the one thing I'll never forget about that trek back across the Llano Estacado is those watermelons.

CHAPTER

★ 22 ★

Having the supplies that Rich Coffee had given us for the rest of the trip made the heat of the day a mite more bearable. Our canteens were constantly full now, as we continued to find the rivers and streams we'd discovered upon leaving Fort Belknap so long ago. Or at least that's how long ago it seemed. This enabled us to make camp at noon and in the evening and cook us up a decent meal of sorts if and when we wanted. Cottonwoods became more frequent in our sightings, the shade of one of them a hell of a lot more desirable for those dry noon camps. Mind you, the heat was still devilish mean and hotter than Hades, there's no mistaking that. It was just a mite more bearable.

We had been six days on the trail when we came to

Fort Chadbourne, a military post that had been occupied by the Union army since the end of the war.

"Want to stop in there and see can we find us a drink?" I asked as we pulled up about three quarters of a mile from the fort. "Damn sure could use one."

"That may be, Chance," Charlie said, "but I'd just as soon have you all sober while I've got this money to look after." When I gave him a frown, he added, "Believe me, boys, when we get to Belknap and I get this gold to a bank that has a guarantee they'll keep it safe for me, why, I'll buy you all the first couple or three rounds of whatever your poison happens to be. But not now."

"He's right, Chance," Wash said. "Your appetite for a drink can wait. Besides, I ain't too fond of those that inhabit the place, if you recall."

"Oh, yeah, I almost forgot." During the war I had fought for the Union and my brother had fought for the Confederacy. In fact, we'd had some real touch-and-go arguments about the war since we got back. The odd thing was we both rode back into town at the same time on the same day.

"What are you grinning about?" Wash asked, suddenly a mite touchy, as though he'd been reading my mind.

"I was remembering the day you and I both rode back into Twin Rifles," I said, still grinning. "Got into a fight in Ernie Johnson's saloon right off. Why, I couldn't remember it was you I was fighting until I heard you bounce off the floor the way you do. There's always been a certain ring to you the way you do that, brother," I teased. I've always been a few inches taller than my younger brother and, if I do say so myself, never let him forget it over the years.

"Knock it off, Chance, or I'll take you apart right here and now," Wash said, trying to put a meanness in his voice I'd heard him only imitate before. Pa always claimed that Wash had more compassion than I did. Maybe that was why he'd gotten married and I hadn't. Who could tell?

"Say, how'd that fight come out?" Emmett asked, leaning forward in his saddle and suddenly taking an interest in our conversation. I reckon the ex-sergeant was a mite like me in that he was always interested in hearing about a good fight.

"We never had a chance to finish it," I said, remembering why all too well.

"Well, how come?"

"Pa found us fighting and beat the hell outta us both," Wash said. I sensed that the toughness had now been replaced by the same sense of reverie I was feeling about that day.

Emmett and Charlie had a chuckle over that, then proceeded to find a decent site for us to make camp. Fort Chadbourne was still in sight but not as close as when we'd first come on it. Still, Wash was feeling awful uncomfortable.

"Can't stand the presence of them Yankees, can you?" I said to my brother when I thought I saw him shiver after we'd eaten our evening meal. "Here, take a warm-up on this stuff," I said and poured the four of us the last of the evening coffee.

"It ain't the Yankees, Chance," Wash said, although I noticed he hadn't refused my offer of coffee. But then you go as long as any one of us had either way across the Llano Estacado and you'd be a fool to turn away anything that was liquid. If you know what I mean.

"Then what is it?" I asked, my feelings changing

181

abruptly from the teasing attitude I'd first had before we'd struck camp to one of genuine concern. I reckon that no matter how many fights you get into with your brother, why, he's still your brother, still blood and kin. And from the uncertainty in Wash's voice I had a notion that what was bothering him wasn't anything to be funning about.

"I don't know, I can't place it exactly," he said, looking down into his coffee. "It's almost like I was being spied on, like I had someone looking over my shoulder who could see everything I was doing."

"I know what you mean, hoss," Emmett said. "Had a touch of it myself earlier. Sent a chill up my spine, I'll tell you that." This had to be serious, for Emmett, who normally had as humorous an outlook as me, wasn't anywhere close to laughing now.

"Don't let it get to you, boys," Charlie said with a smile. "Hell, you're both married men. Your mind's likely getting you ready to being bossed around worse than I ever done you on the trail."

Charlie and me laughed, but were quickly interrupted by a thoroughly serious-faced Wash.

"No it ain't," he said, a frown coming to his forehead. "Someone's out there watching us."

All of a sudden the conversation dried up quicker than a lone raindrop at high noon on the Llano. But then why shouldn't it? After all, we had twelve thousand dollars in gold with us.

There was something eerie about coming awake in a world of darkness the next morning. All I could think was it had to be Wash and those scary words he'd spoken last night. It was almost as though you could see ghosts everywhere, even though your mind knew better. I reckon it was one of those days when your nerves take over your feelings and rule damn near everything. Sort of like the day after All Hallows Eve, if you know what I mean.

Breakfast was made in a quiet manner and eaten in silence. Why, you'd have thought the whole meal was being eaten in the middle of a graveyard. And I'll tell you, hoss, I didn't think I was exaggerating at the time either.

"Ain't this the seventh day we've been on the trail?" Charlie asked as we mounted up that morning.

"Yeah, I reckon it is," Emmett said after doing some figuring in his head. "Why do you ask?"

"I thought seven was supposed to be a lucky number."

"So I hear." Emmett again.

"That being the case, let's not ride into Belknap like some kind of funeral procession," Charlie said. "It would embarrass the hell outta me," he added as he put the spurs to his mount, his mule in tow.

Ever since quitting our mules, we'd been riding our horses. No one had said spit about changing back to the mules. I reckon it was a unanimous silent agreement that those mules were nothing more than a last resort as long as we had decent horse flesh to ride now. Besides, what with having some provisions along again, why, it just seemed more sensible to try and enjoy our trek back to Belknap now that we were past the Llano Estacado.

We were just finishing up our dry camp at noon when all hell broke loose.

"Looks like you were right, Wash," I said as I looked up at the horses drawing nearer and nearer our camp.

"Can't be Indians," Emmett said.

"That's for damn sure. We've been in Comanche country ever since we reached the Lower Concho," I said. "Hell, they'd be on us by now, if they was Comanch'."

"Something about 'em looks familiar," Charlie was saying as he pulled his six-gun and checked his loads. Me, I was doing the same when it crossed my mind that I still had that second Colt strapped to my left side. I was suddenly glad it was.

"I'll say," I said in agreement. They had gotten closer and closer, riding at what appeared to be an easy lope, just taking their time to come to us. "Don't look none too sociable either," I added. Like I say, they were getting closer and I'd recognized them, the whole lot.

"Goddamn if it ain't them Unionists," Charlie growled, recognizing them too. I didn't think it would take him long to identify the crowd who had stolen some of our cattle. I took a quick count as they rode up, tallying fifteen, maybe more.

"Yeah, it's the Goodnight bunch," one of them said as they reined in their horses in front of us. The horses and mules had quickly been moved to the side. Provided we came out of this fracas still walking, I also wanted to still be able to ride my horse and you can't very well do that when either you or the horse is dead as can be. "Didn't surprise you, did we?" he added, trying to be some kind of smart ass.

It didn't work.

We stood side by side, about two feet apart from one another, each of us with a holstered pistol at his side, me with two. And these fools wanted to open the ball.

"Hell, no!" Charlie snarled. "How could someone

surprise you when you can smell 'em two miles away?" The whole lot of them were still dressed in nothing but dirty, filthy clothing, the same as the first time we'd come on them.

That got the talker's eyes wide open real quick.

"I see you boys still ain't learned how to bathe or change into a decent set of clothes every once in a while," I said, giving the bunch of them a good wide grin as I spoke. I noticed the talker was getting madder, at least if the look of him was any hint.

"Just what is it you came for, mister?" Charlie said, the scowl still on his face. "I know it wasn't to jaw about the weather."

"Ain't no money in talking 'bout that, friend," the man said. His own grin widened then as he said, "I come for your money."

This surprised Charlie as much as the rest of us, I reckon. "How in the hell did you know about that?"

"Been tracking you for the last three days, Goodnight. Knew you'd come back with a pouch full of money from selling those mangy longhorns. Now, how 'bout saving us all a lot of trouble and handing it over?"

"Not hardly," Charlie said with a firm voice.

"Oughtta make you feel better, Wash, knowing you got good senses and not a case of the spooks," I said to my brother.

"Yeah. I'll remember those words of wisdom, Chance." I could tell he was a mite on the skittish side, likely about the number of *hombres* we were facing and the handful of us who were facing them.

"Now, Wash, you ain't doubtful about this bunch of long-necked buzzards, are you?" I said, talking to him as though it were a private conversation with no one

185

else around. "Why, you ain't forget that band of Comancheros we took on, are you? The ones that killed Ma just as we come back from the war? Twice as mean as this bunch here, and we took care of 'em like they was nothing, I remember that for a fact." I sure did. I'd charged into camp like a fool, both guns blazing, and got shot up my own self in the process. But Wash and Pa and me, we'd done in that whole bunch of killers. "This crowd of saddle stiffs ain't gonna give us no trouble."

I reckon if there was one thing I could have said that got the lot of them fired up it was that last sentence. Bug-eyed? Why, you don't get that kind of expression on a man's face unless you kick him in the elsewheres. Or call him worthless, which is just what I'd done to every one of these yahoos.

"You got an awful loud mouth, mister," the talker said.

"And you ain't the first one to ever say it," was my reply. I still grinned like hell, enjoying every minute of it. "Hell, my brother tells me that all the time."

"Better git off them hosses, boys," Emmett said, cool as could be. I got the notion he was like a youngster in the candy store. He'd found a good fight and he was going to be in it and he couldn't ask for better than that. But then that was Emmett for you.

"What the hell for?" another of the crowd spoke up defiantly.

"I reckon he don't want no one saying we took advantage of you after we kill you all," Wash said. I can't tell you how good it was to hear my brother spout off like that. I knew then he'd give as good as he got that day and that was that.

"Now, let me get this straight," Charlie said. "You

come to rob me, is that it? Come for my gold, you said?"

The talker looked at Charlie like he was round the bend. "Mister, are you deaf or stupid, or what? Hell, yes, that's what I said I come for."

"Just wanted to get the story right so I know what to tell the local law when I come across 'em and tell 'em why it is I left a worthless bunch of bastards like you out here for buzzard bait."

Once again the talker's eyes bugged out.

"Bug Eye," I said, addressing the supposed leader of this group of yahoos, "I'm tired of talking. If you come here to do some, then do it or turn them horses around and get the hell out of here. Besides, I think you're a bunch of goddamn cowards anyway." I figured that if anything would get them moving being called a coward would.

It did.

"Why, you—" the talker started to say as he brought his rifle down out of the crook of his arm. He never made it any farther than that.

By the time he had it close to a throw-down position, I'd already pulled out both of my Colts and fired a shot each at him and the man on his right. Both shots were true to their mark and the two of them were dead as they toppled from their mounts.

I worked the actions on both Colts as fast as I could, firing one shot then another, missing only twice before one of the guns was empty and the other had only one shot left. By then, I noticed that three of these fellows had no stomach for a fight at all. I can verify that for I saw them hightail it out of there as soon as the shooting started. By the time the gunsmoke cleared, they were nowhere in sight.

Wash wasn't as fast as me, but he was accurate at the shooting he did, and for what he was doing that was what counted most. I think he fired four shots and put three more of the would-be thieves out of their misery as their horses got a mite more than skittish. In the process, I thought I saw him jerk back some, then saw a patch of red start to spread high in his chest. He'd been hit but he wasn't about to stop. By God, that was my brother they were tangling with!

Emmett shot the two on the far left out of their saddles, apparently only wounding one of them, for when they hit the ground one of them got back up and charged Emmett. The ex-sergeant shot the once wounded man and he wasn't wounded any more. He was dead. His third shot misfired for some reason, and that put him between a rock and a hard spot, for the man on his horse also had a rifle and was about to bring it down on Emmett and kill him. I used my last shot to shoot the rifle out of the man's hands and that gave Emmett all the chance he needed. With one of his big fists, he grabbed the horseman and pulled him out of the saddle and commenced to beat the hell out of him with his pistol, likely drawing more blood than if he would have shot the son of a bitch. But like I say, that was Emmett.

Charlie Goodnight, well, he wasn't no gunman, that was for sure. But he did know how to use a six-gun, I'll say that for him. I remembered him originally telling these same Unionists that if they wanted to send all the men they couldn't use anymore to come after him, for when he got through with them, they wouldn't be coming back. Well, hoss, the two men he shot up weren't going no place but to hell by the time he was through with them. I do believe he would have shot a third but that last man, too, had no stomach for killing and put the spurs to his horse as soon as the shooting began.

So there we stood, battered and a mite shot up, but we were still standing.

That is, until Wash passed out.

CHAPTER
★ 23 ★

You done fine, Wash, just fine," I said after I'd worked the slug out of the high part of my brother's chest.

The gunsmoke had cleared not long after the shooting stopped and sure enough, we counted eleven dead men laying about, their horses scattered everywhere from the sound of the gunfire. Ten of them had been shot to death by the four of us, while one of them had died a nasty death from Emmett as the ex-sergeant beat the man to death with his six-gun. The only thing Emmett seemed to regret was the fact that his pistol wasn't worth a damn any more.

Charlie Goodnight rounded up some of the horses while Emmett mounted his own and went after those who'd scattered farther away. I got the fire going a mite hotter than it had been and dug through my own saddlebags looking for medicinals and rags and such I was pretty sure I didn't have. Still, I had to be doing something. I suppose I could have reloaded my Colts, but I was too worried about Wash and the gunshot he'd taken to be of much use doing that at the moment. Mind you, I'd done my fair share of bandaging during the war, but there was something about having to fix up one of your own, someone like your own brother, that made it a good deal harder to do. Finally, I just settled for picking up one of the handguns that hadn't been fired by one of the dead men and sticking it in my waistband. I reckon it was when Charlie Goodnight came across a bottle of rotgut whiskey in one of the dead men's saddlebags that I felt a good deal of relief.

"Think you can use this?" he asked as he approached me.

"Damn sure betcha," I said and snatched the bottle from his hand. I uncorked it and took a good long pull on it, damn near losing my voice as the fiery liquid passed down my gullet. When I had a semblance of a voice back in my throat, I said, "He's gonna need it too," and pointed toward Wash, who still lay there unconscious.

"But not as bad as you just did, I'll bet," Charlie said.

"Betcher ass," was all I could think to say.

The brand of poison I'd just swallowed could have been Triple X for all I knew. Whatever it was it settled my nerves enough to approach Wash and do my damnedest taking that bullet out. I'd poured some of the whiskey over the bowie knife I carried at my side, hoping it would serve as an antiseptic of sorts. Men had died of infection more than the bullets they'd been shot with out here, that much I was aware of, and I didn't want it to happen to my brother. Hell, how would I explain it to his wife? I reckon I was lucky in getting the bullet out for it didn't seem to have gone that far into the man. Or maybe I was getting better at this frontier surgery than I knew. I didn't know, nor did I care at the time. It was after I'd laid my knife on the fire to draw some heat and then slapped it on Wash's wound that I felt a good deal of comfort within me. It even seemed as though I could stand the terrible smell of burnt flesh rising from my brother's wound. Ain't nothing like it in the world, that I can guarantee you, hoss. Or maybe it was because Wash let out the goddamnedest yell I'd ever heard a Rebel make.

"What the hell are you smiling at, you simple bastard!" he yelled at me, trying to get up and then falling right back down on his back.

That was when I said, "You done fine, Wash, just fine."

"You damn near killed me!" he yelled again, still madder than a wet hen.

"No he didn't," Charlie said, looking at Wash with raised eyebrow, "he just saved your life, friend."

That left my brother a mite speechless. Or maybe it was the fact that he didn't like being beholden to anyone anymore than I did that made him hold his tongue.

"Don't worry, brother," I said with a smile, "I won't shove it down your throat." Not any more than a couple of times, at least, I thought to myself silently, which made me grin that much more.

"You know, Chance, you took a bullet or so too," Charlie said by way of observation. "Unless, of course, you've been scratching your side while you worked on your brother there."

I gave a quick glance down at my left side, and sure enough I'd been shot about the same place I'd just gotten knifed at by that damned Apache not two weeks ago. But just as the Apache hadn't cut deep enough, the bullet hadn't either and this turned out to be little more than a crease.

"I reckon Shorty was right," Charlie said a few minutes later as he patched up my side and wound some more bandages around my chest and side. "You have taken more than a couple of bullets in your time." He'd lifted my shirt up over my back to do his patching and apparently seen scars that can only be left by bullet wounds. I wasn't going to tell the man, but if he could see below my belt line, he'd also find a handful of scars in my thighs and legs.

"You know, Charlie, I give that some thought oncet," I said after he'd made his remark.

"What's that?"

"If I'd saved all the lead that's been taken out of me, why, if they ever got a market for it like that gold and silver those miners are always hungering for, I could retire a rich man if I cashed it all in."

"Know what you mean, Chance, know what you mean," he replied with a smile.

I reckon a man never really figures he'll wind up feeling like a pin cushion again, especially after he's been shot a time or two. Me, I'd been used for more target practice than anyone else I'd known. Of course, Pa would say it was all my fault, me being the fighter that I am. And I reckon if I give it a good long bit of thought I might even agree. But then no man wants to admit he's wrong, not even to himself.

Emmett rode back into camp about then, herding along a handful of horses that had gotten away during the shooting. "Say, don't drink that all in one swig, Chance," he said as he dismounted. "Save some for a thirsty man, will you?"

"Sure," I all but whispered, feeling the tightness of Charlie's bandaging on my chest as I took my breath nice and easy for a while. I handed him the bottle and he took a long pull on it, just like the old-time sergeant I knew he was. Sergeants in the army were some of the hardest drinkers I'd ever come across in my life, of that I was certain. Seeing Emmett take as long a pull as he did just reaffirmed my belief.

Wash said he was awful sore, so I tried to explain to him where I thought the bullet I'd taken out of him was. He'd been hit high in the chest, but the bullet hadn't gone anywhere near his heart or lungs that I could tell. Not being a bona fide physician, I figured this all out for myself because he was still breathing normal, and what blood was left in his system had been pumping hard enough to get him excited about being cauterized by my bowie knife the way he had. No dead man ever yells that loud, I can tell you.

"When you feel well enough, put that shirt on," I said and tossed a spare I'd fished out of his saddlebags down beside him. "The slug's in the pocket if you want to impress Sarah Ann," I added with a smile.

"All I want to do is hold her," Wash said.

"Don't blame you one bit," I said. I was beginning to get an urge to hold Rachel Ferris in my arms when we returned too. Or is it coming that close to death that makes you want to hold on to someone you're fond of like that? Hell, I didn't know.

We found enough material to fashion a sling for Wash to put his left arm in for a while as he began to heal. If he didn't, he'd likely start bleeding again, and I simply wasn't fond of patching people up. I didn't mind shooting a man who deserved it, mind you, it was just all that blood that flowed afterward that made things overly messy.

There was still some daylight left so we saddled up and headed for the nearest water hole to bed down for the night, taking our time as we did. It wasn't just that Wash and me had been shot so much as the fact that we also had most of the horses that those yahoos fool enough to tangle with us had been shot out of.

Emmett and Charlie did right fine tending to the chores in camp that night while my brother and I took it easy for a change. The following day we were back at Fort Belknap, and I don't believe I was ever happier to see civilization than that day. Charlie made a stop at the bank then took us all to the local eatery and ordered us all a good thick cut of beef steak, panfried and all.

"May you never eat rattlesnake again," he said as he took his first sip of coffee, speaking the words as though they were some kind of toast.

"None of us," Emmett said.

To which I added, "Amen, brother."

As hungry as we were, I figure the meal took longer to cook than it did to eat. When the waitress had filled our cups for the last time, Charlie reached inside his jacket pocket and pulled out a piece of paper, spreading it out on the table for us all to see. It was a bank check from him and it was made out to Emmett, Wash, and me. The amount of the check was twelve hundred dollars.

"That's a lot of cash to be carrying around, even for a handful of *hombres* tough as you three," he said. "You give that to your banker back in Twin Rifles and he'll deposit it for you after you three each sign the back of it. That's for the remuda you sold me."

"Thanks, Charlie," each of us said and each stuck a paw out to shake his hand, as though it concluded our business deal. I reckon it wasn't much more than a formality, for the lot of us had come to know and trust one another. You don't go through the hard times we had and not get to feel that way about one another in one way, shape, or form.

"Are you sure you don't want to give it a second go with me?" Charlie asked, only half smiling when he said it, as though he were teasing us in the asking. "I can still use three good men like you boys."

"A second trip?" I asked in near astonishment.

"Yeah. I told Oliver I'd see if I couldn't round up some more longhorns and take a second herd out before the snow flies." He said it as though it were nothing, as though he'd done the whole thing a hundred times before. Me, go back across that godforsaken Llano Estacado? I'm laughing!

"Not a chance, Charlie," Emmett said for all of us. "We all got women waiting for us back in Twin Rifles, and it's been too long since we've seen 'em."

"You understand, don't you?" Wash asked.

"Sure," Charlie smiled, this time a genuine one. "Just thought I'd ask."

At this point Charlie reached back in his pocket and pulled out some paper money and began counting out the bills into three piles.

"There's two hundred dollars for each of you," he said with a good deal of pride. I got the idea he didn't pay these kind of wages to most of his men.

"The last time I saw that kind of money was on a wanted poster of some scoundrel in Pa's office," I said, not stretching the truth one bit.

We must have thanked Charlie Goodnight in a real profuse manner, for we wound up buying him a couple of drinks afterward.

The next day we struck out for Twin Rifles. We all decided to take our time getting back, as much as we all wanted to see the women again. But Wash couldn't ride all that hard without opening that wound of his, and after a while I got to feeling a mite light in the head too, so the rest would do us good.

"Something bothering you, Chance?" Wash asked when part of our morning ride had passed.

Something was indeed bothering me. It had first struck me after I'd pulled the bullet out of Wash that day of the gunfight. It had stuck in the back of my mind that something wasn't right that day. Something about those Unionist characters we'd had the run-in with. There was something strange about them, something that was missing. It had been eating at me ever since, until this morning, that is. Then it had come to me. Then I knew. And that bothered me more, which is why Wash must have noticed the look of concern on my face.

"Nothing, Wash," I said to him. "It's just this goddamn bandage. It seems too tight at times."

Hell, you didn't think I was going to tell my brother that the flannelmouth who called himself Fredericks wasn't with those Unionists when they showed up, did you? Why, Wash would ride hell-for-leather for Sarah Ann just to make sure she was all right. And likely bust open that wound of his in the process.

And what good's a brother to you if he's dead?

CHAPTER

★ 24 ★

Like I say, we took our time getting back. By the fourth day Wash and I were both feeling a whole lot more feisty than we had been when we'd left Fort Belknap. You can chalk it off to rest or just plain old Mother Nature taking her course with Father Time, take your pick. Either way the both of us had healed a lot faster than either figured we would. Of course, in Wash's case I was sure it was more the wanting to be a fit man for the day he got back to his Sarah Ann than anything else that drove him to healing as quick as he did. But then I reckon a woman will do that to a man, especially a married woman who lays claim to being your wife. Come to think of it, I'd been having some real spicy notions about Rachel Ferris of late and how badly I was wanting to kiss her once I returned. As for Emmett, well, I reckon his biggest chore was babysitting us for those three days. I say three days because on the fourth day he'd about had it.

"All right, you loafers," he said in all but a yell that morning, sounding very much like he'd stepped right into his old rank as a cavalry sergeant. But then I reckon he'd likely never stepped out of it, truth to tell. "You know just as well as I do that ain't either of you sick or ailing anymore."

I reckon we had been taking a good deal for granted as he'd waited on us damn near hand and foot those past three days. And he was right, both Wash and I were feeling a mite better now.

"But Emmett, we're still wounded men," Wash said, acting like he had that first day he'd been shot. "You ain't gonna turn down your comrades in arms, are you?" I knew what my brother was doing, could see right through his scheme of things, likely because I was doing the same thing.

"Oh, horse apples," the cavalryman said with a stern frown.

"Better listen to him, Emmett," I said in what I thought to be a serious tone of voice. "Why, the lad's still looking mighty peaked, if you ask me."

But Emmett wasn't having any today. The furrow that formed in his brow was so deep it could have been put there by an old Missouri mule, I thought.

"Well, I ain't *asking* you, boys, I'm a-telling you!" he said in his best sergeant's tone. "Now, you two pilgrims better start gathering wood and fixing me some coffee, or I'm likely to lose my temper something fierce." And with that he plunked himself down under the cottonwood we'd made camp near and waited for his orders to be carried out.

That was the morning Wash and me forgot our little

con over Emmett and started riding tall in the saddle again.

"There," Emmett said as we broke camp and he rode out behind us, "now you're looking like the Carston boys I come to know."

"Tell me something, Emmett," I said over my shoulder.

"If I can."

"Do you tell Greta what to do like this?"

"Hell no!" he said in an emphatic manner. "Why, being away from home's the first time I've felt like a sergeant since I got married. Honest."

"You mean Greta orders you around in your own house?" Wash asked incredulously.

"Taken over the house like an old sergeant major I used to have, she did," Emmett said. "Believe it or not, Wash, sooner or later they all do," he added on a sad note.

When I saw Wash's eyes open wide with what looked like fear, I smiled and said, "That's why I'm still a bachelor, boys."

The fourth day was also the day we rode into Twin Rifles. Like Charlie Goodnight had, we made our first stop at the bank. The three of us signed the back of that bank check Goodnight had given us and told the bank manager to divvy it up three ways and put eight hundred dollars in the account Wash and I had and four hundred dollars in Emmett's account, which is how the three of us had agreed to do it. A frugal man could make a decent living off of those kind of savings for damn near a decade if he watched how he spent his money. Then we stopped in and saw Pa, who was seated behind his desk and glad to see we'd at least made it back alive, if not in the best of conditions.

"Say, I'm glad you boys had the good sense to stop by and see me," he said once we'd finished shaking hands and greeting one another. I thought I detected a note of concern in his voice as he spoke.

"How's that, Pa?" I asked, knowing that Pa didn't say things like that out of sheer folly.

Pa told us how he'd been out to our place one Sunday for dinner with Sarah Ann and a stranger had ridden up, claiming to be looking for me. He'd done a right keen job of scaring Sarah Ann out of her wits before Pa had sent the man packing.

"That was when I sent Joshua to do some checking on that *hombre* for me," he said. Joshua was the deputy Pa had helping him out who did a lot of filling in and extra things when the need be. For a man who'd come out of the hills somewhere back yonder, Joshua had a fairly good command of the language and could get by without sounding like he knew nothing; something all of us Carstons had learned not long after meeting the deputy. "Picked up his name from Ernie over at the saloon and decided to check him out, even though he wasn't on one of my posters for being wanted." The telegraph hadn't come to Twin Rifles yet so Joshua had ridden clear to San Antonio to find out the information Pa had wanted.

"Big man?" I asked. "Face full of beard as black as his eyes."

"And likely his soul," Pa said, "if what Joshua found out is true."

"And?" Wash was getting antsy now. I could tell it in his voice, see it in his eyes. If that wasn't fear for Sarah Ann's safety, I don't know what it was.

"His name's Fredericks," I said, feeling certain I knew the man as the same one Charlie Goodnight and

I'd had a run-in with up around Fort Belknap, the same one who'd led those Unionists we'd just finished tangling with.

Pa nodded. "J. D. Fredericks. He's killed men, they say."

That was all Wash and Emmett needed before the two of them turned tail and ran like hell out the entrance to the jail. Likely making their way to see if they still had wives that were good and healthy, especially with the likes of this Fredericks character around.

"Now, what got into them?" Pa asked in a puzzled manner.

"It's one of them long stories, Pa."

"Then give me the short version."

"If he's the man I'm thinking he is, I had a run-in with him after we got those horses up to Charlie Goodnight at Fort Belknap," I told Pa. "This Fredericks was heading up a group calling themselves Unionists. Turns out they stole some of Goodnight's cattle, upwards of seventy head, as I recall. Fredericks didn't like being called on it and said he'd get both Charlie and me."

"You figure that's how he showed up down here? Hunting you down?"

"Yeah."

"What about these Unionists he was leading? Why didn't he bring them with him?"

"Must figure he can do me in by himself," I said. "As for the Unionists, they ain't no more."

Pa cocked a curious eye toward me. "They *ain't?*"

"A dozen or so of 'em tried taking twelve thousand dollars off Emmett, Wash, Charlie Goodnight, and me. We worked too hard to let 'em have it without a fight. I reckon there's at least a dozen, maybe a mite shy of that number who ain't with the Unionists no more."

"I get the drift of your story, son."

All the time I'd relayed the story, I'd been checking my loads, once again aware that I had both of my Colts on my gun belt. Once again I found myself glad I did, for as I'd retold my story I'd begun to remember something that had totally escaped me until now.

"I'd better go after Wash," I said, sliding my Colt back in its holster. "He still ain't in all that good a shape to go fighting some big battle."

Pa was strapping on his own six-gun as I spoke. "You help your brother out and I'll check with Ernie Johnson and see ary I can find this Fredericks fella. If he's in town, he'll be in jail by the time you get back. You can count on it."

"I know. Thanks, Pa," I said as I headed out the door, then stopped in my tracks and turned to face him again. "One other thing, Pa."

"What's that?"

"Three or four of those Unionists beat a hasty retreat once the shooting started back there. I don't know where they went, but I'd lay odds they ain't got enough brains to do much thinking on their own."

"Figure they might show up where this trouble-maker does?"

"That's exactly what I'm thinking."

"I'll keep that in mind, son."

I bumped into Dallas Bodeen on the way to my horse, which was still hitched in front of the bank.

"Boy, am I glad to see you, Chance," the old-timer said. He was one of Pa's old friends from his days with the Texas Rangers and he'd stuck around after he and Pa and Wash had an adventure of some sort with the Comanches up north. I never did get the gist of the whole story, but like a lot of things I reckon it was a whole 'nother canyon.

"Ain't got time to talk, Dallas," I said in a hurried manner as I climbed atop my tired old mount. "See Pa over at the jail, maybe you can help him out."

I don't know what kind of response that got, for I was reining my horse and kicking his sides by the time I was through speaking. If I knew Wash, he'd likely pull something that I was more used to me doing. But then he was a married man and love will do strange things to you, especially when it's new. Even more so when it's a woman you call your wife, I reckon. So my brother would ride into the jaws of Hades if that was what it took to keep Sarah Ann safe. He might get killed doing it, but he'd do it just the same. Like I said, that's love.

Our ranch house was only a couple of miles from town, so I knew I'd be there in a matter of minutes. That didn't give me an awful lot of time to formulate some kind of plan, but then I reckon I do some of my best fighting that way, thinking things out as they happen. Wash and Pa, well, they were a lot better planners than me, but I was still alive so you wouldn't find me belittling myself over the way I did or didn't do things. All I had to know was that my Colts were fully loaded and how much wind was in the air so I'd shoot my straightest. After that just let me at them! Believe me, when I was through with them, they'd know who they'd been tangling with. And I say that without any sort of brag attached to it!

I reined in my mount just before reaching the back of the barn, not sure if anyone would hear me coming or not. If Wash had already been done in, I was likely somebody's target practice once I rounded the corner.

If, on the other hand, there was a heated argument going on, well, hoss, if you've ever been in one of those, you ought to know you barely hear the other fellow talking much less whatever else is going on around you. I know, I've been in more than one of them.

There was an argument going on all right. From what I could see as I carefully stuck my head around the side of the barn, Sarah Ann was all but glued to Wash's side, her husband's arm around her as though it would keep her safe. Wash was doing the arguing and he was doing it with two men I thought I vaguely recognized as two of the Unionists who'd cut and run when their friends had been counting on them. Wash was about to take on the both of them, but I knew he couldn't do it, not against two armed men like these. It was time to deal myself in on this hand. I'd never be able to forgive myself if I didn't. And neither would Wash. As I stepped out from the side of the barn, I found myself hoping against hope that Pa had found Fredericks and the fourth man in town.

"I told you, Chance ain't here and I ain't seen your friend Fredericks," Wash said, not a quiver in his voice. I had a notion he knew what he was up against, but like I said, he was a married man now and he'd go through hell for that woman beside him. I reckon I would too if I was in his place. "You best get out of here before you regret it."

"Don't make me laugh, sonny," one of them said in what came close to being a guttural laugh. They were about to take on my brother, but I couldn't let them do that.

"If you don't want to take him seriously, *amigo*, then maybe you oughtta turn around and try me," I said, stepping off to the side so I wouldn't be shooting at Wash and Sarah Ann instead of these two yahoos.

"And who the hell are you?" the second one asked as the two turned to face me.

"Oh, that's right," I said, putting on a wide grin again, just like I had with their friends when we'd taken them on. "You two only saw me briefly."

"What?"

"Well, the only part of you that was facing me was your sorry ass while you hightailed it from that fight we had with your friends. At least they died fighting," I said evenly. "Believe me, if there's one thing I've discovered about the likes of you two, it's that you ain't reliable at all. No, sir."

If you want to start a fight with someone, hoss, just insult the hell out of them. Ain't nothing that will rile a man more than some inkling that he's of a cowardly nature. I'd all but done that with these two.

It was enough.

Like what usually takes place when all hell breaks loose, it all happened at one time. The two would-be gunmen in front of me both went for their guns. But would-be gunmen was as far as they'd ever rate on this earth. Fact of the matter is, it was the last thing they did this earth. I drew both my Colts at one time, fired both at one time. Both bullets struck their intended victims in the chest, knocking them backwards. I fired two more shots into their chests, just in case I hadn't hit their hearts with the first.

Wash must have seen something over my shoulder, for he pushed Sarah Ann off to his left as he moved to his right, all the while drawing his six-gun and firing. I turned around as he fired, only to see the man called Fredericks fall from the hayloft door, dropping the rifle in his hand as he did. I could tell by the quickly spreading red pattern on his shirt front that my brother had done him in with just one shot. That was Wash, always saving his ammunition.

But as it turned out, it wasn't just Wash who had shot Fredericks. As soon as I saw him hit the ground, I saw Dallas Bodeen drop the smoking Henry rifle from his shoulder as he moved a few more feet out from the side of the barn he'd apparently been hiding near. All it took was two steps out and he'd had a clear shot of the man who would no longer scare the bejesus out of Sarah Ann.

"Wash already had him in his sights," I said to Dallas. "Why'd you shoot him?"

"It ain't that I doubt your brother's aim, Chance," Dallas said. "I just never liked the bastard." Dallas slowly shook his head, as though taking pity on the dead man. "I reckon he was handy." He showed a firm grip of his rifle, shaking it in the air like I'd seen many a warrior do, as he added, "But then so was I."

"What the hell's going on?" I heard Emmett say as he pulled in the reins of his horse, suddenly appearing in our yard. He'd come from the direction of his own house, so I could only assume that Greta and the kids were fine.

"Had a mite of gunplay here," Wash said, Sarah Ann back in his arms now.

"I'll say," Emmett said, taking in the sight of the dead men.

But it wasn't over yet.

The fourth man, the one I'd all but forgotten about, suddenly appeared out of the barn door. He must have been hiding inside all the while, still afraid to take part in the fight. But somehow he'd turned into a desperate man, for as he stood boldly in the open now, he brought his rifle up and took aim at Emmett, who was totally surprised.

"Sonofabitch!" the big ex-sergeant exclaimed as the bullet struck his leg. It was a reflex action that brought Emmett's pistol out and in his hand in no longer than it took to bat your eye. He fired at the last man while the killer was cocking his rifle, but Emmett's aim was true and he hit the man in the stomach.

I'd holstered my own guns and found myself drawing them again. There'd been enough killing today, and if doing in this one last man would keep any more from happening, then I'd help finish the man off. At the same time I shot him, Dallas Bodeen put another slug from his Henry rifle into the man. I only hoped the man was prepared to die, for he had no chance of living with all that lead in him now. He slumped to the ground, dead.

"I hope that's the last of them," I heard Sarah Ann say, a bit of fear in her voice. Not that I could blame her.

"Look at it this way, Sarah Ann," I said, still trying to smile. "If nothing else happens in your life, why, someday you'll have a story to tell your grandchildren."

"Chance," Wash said in a serious tone, "just shut up and get this mess cleaned up."

"Me?" I said in astonishment.

"Hell, yes. You'll likely claim you made most of it anyway."

Brothers!

CHAPTER

★ 25 ★

Dallas and me loaded the four bodies into the buckboard and headed for the town undertaker, who also
doubled as the town carpenter when the need arose. It
could be amazing how many skills a man discovered
he had out here, purely amazing. Dallas did some
quick fix-up work on Emmett's leg, and the big man
rode along with us, making his stop at the doctor's
office to get his wound taken care of. I had an idea that
Emmett was a lot like me in that he'd been shot up a
time or two and didn't do much more than grit his
teeth a lot as he headed for the local physician. As for
Wash, I left him with Sarah Ann, figuring the two of
them would need the time alone to talk over what had
happened while the other was gone. Of course, they

being married and all, I had a strong suspicion the two of them might just leave the talking until later. And believe me, fixing a meal for Wash was likely the last thing on Sarah Ann's mind. From listening to men like Emmett, I'd found out there was a whole lot that can be said between a couple of married folk without either of them whispering so much as a word.

After getting rid of the dead men, Dallas and me stopped by Pa's office and offered to buy him supper. He agreed and we headed for the Ferris House while Joshua, who'd just ridden back into town from taking care of a dispute at a local farm, said he'd watch the office while Pa was gone.

"You just tell them Ferris women to save me a chunk of whatever it is they's serving for supper," he added in a serious tone. "I gotta eat too, you know."

Pa nodded, smiling. "I'll make sure Chance don't eat the whole hog," he said as we left.

Supper turned out to be roast beef. Now, you might think that after eating as much beef as I had—boiled or otherwise—I'd balk at the serving up of one more portion. But these Ferris women could cook up a storm and do a right fine job of it, so I wasn't about to complain. Not at all. I'd learned the hard way that these two put a lot of faith in the sign they'd posted above the entrance to the kitchen area of their boardinghouse: *Annoying the cook will result in smaller portions being served.*

"Say, Miss Margaret," I said when the three of us had finished our meal and Margaret Ferris was pouring us one last cup of coffee. "Do you think I could get a room with you all tonight?"

"Oh?" Margaret looked at me in a quizzical way. "I thought you and Wash had a place just outside of town?"

I felt a mite of red crawling up my neck as I said, "Well, we do, ma'am, but it's been a while since Wash and Sarah Ann seen one another and . . ." My words trailed off as I wasn't sure how to end the sentence or finish saying what I was saying. It's one of those things a man doesn't often get cause to explain.

But Margaret was soon there to rescue me. Smiling, she said, "I think I know what you mean, Chance. And I'm sure we've got an extra room Rachel can fix up for you."

"Thank you, ma'am. I appreciate it."

Margaret was about to walk off when she stopped, as though a thought had struck her and she might as well get it out before she forgot about it. "Of course, I still expect you to pay for it. The room, I mean."

"Oh, yes, ma'am," I said. "That drive we went on paid off real handsome. I can pay the going rate, yes, ma'am."

She stood there a minute thinking something over. "I'll tell you what, Chance, your Pa hasn't paid me one red cent since he's been staying here and I still manage to get a good trade for what we agree on." I knew that Pa had agreed to chop wood each morning for the use of his room and a couple of meals at the Ferris House, so all of a sudden I was curious as to just what Margaret Ferris had in mind for me.

"Well, I don't know, Miss Margaret," I said uncertainly. "I don't know if I could chop you much wood, this side of mine being cut up and shot and all."

"Oh, I understand," she replied. Again she was taking that thinking look back into her mind. Then she had the solution, just like always it seemed. "I know, why don't you give Rachel a hand with the dishes?"

"Dishes?" I said and damn near lost my voice over

that one word. Why, I didn't even do dishes out at the ranch!

"Actually, what I was thinking was that you could help Rachel by drying the dishes for her," Margaret said, amending her original statement. When she saw the troubled look on my face, she smiled and added, "I know Rachel has been asking all sorts of questions about that drive you and Wash were on. I'm sure you could talk to her if you want to pass the time of day."

I don't often have an abrupt change of thought, but I'd been wanting to talk to Rachel my own self, so maybe this was my chance. I gave Margaret my best smile. "All right. For you I'll do it, Miss Margaret."

I don't know why Dallas was looking at Pa and shaking his head as I left the room. I reckon you never can tell about those old-timers. Must be being around too long or something.

Rachel was all smiles when I entered the kitchen. I explained what her mother wanted me to do, and she handed me a towel and went back to washing the evening meal's dishes. You could bet I was never going to tell Wash about this little episode.

She wanted to know all about the drive with the longhorns and all so I told her about the heat and the Llano Estacado and the trail we'd blazed. I didn't mention the men who'd died along the way, much less the cattle who'd done the same. I'd always thought of Rachel as one of those women who was real genteel about things, if you know what I mean, so I spared her the harsh details.

"You know, Chance, I kind of missed you while you were gone," Rachel said when I'd quieted down some, having finished my story. I wondered if she felt as uneasy about saying those words as I did about having to reply to them.

I could feel that red crawling up my neck again as I tried to find the right words to say. "Yeah, me too. I mean, I missed you too while I was gone."

It was when I said those words that Rachel stopped washing her dishes and began wiping her hands off on the apron she wore, draped from her neck. I had a sudden urge to run like hell, sure that I'd have had better luck with the Comanche Nation than I'd have with this woman.

"Are you through with the dishes?" I asked, feeling stupid for saying what I did when I saw the stack of dirty pots and pans yet to be washed.

"Actually, I was just beginning," Rachel said with a smile in what I thought to be a purposeful manner. Two steps was all that separated us and she took them, placing her arms around my neck and gently pulling my face down to hers, offering up a kiss just as gentle as the woman.

"Yes, ma'am, I'd say you are," I said when our lips parted. To say that I was surprised would be putting it mildly, for the woman had never done such a thing to me before.

It was then I thought I saw Pa standing by that kitchen entrance. Just about the time I saw him, he was yanked away, by Margaret Ferris as it turned out.

"Will Carston, you get away from there and leave those two youngsters be," I heard her tell Pa in a loud whisper.

"I wonder if that boy knows what he's getting into?" I heard Pa say. I knew that Rachel was hearing the same thing, and when I looked at her I saw that she too was smiling at the words of her mother and my pa.

"Believe me, Will, what those two are getting into is nothing you or I will ever be able to do anything about. Now let's leave them alone."

Then they were gone.

I looked at Rachel and didn't feel the fear that had enveloped me only a few minutes before. I wasn't sure I knew why or even how it had come about. All I knew was I had enjoyed kissing this woman.

I smiled at her. "You said something about just beginning?"

She smiled back at me, saying, "As a matter of fact, I did."

Then she kissed me again and I don't mind telling you I liked it. Liked it a lot as I took her in my arms.

You see what I mean?

There are some things you can get across to another person without saying a hell of a lot at all.

Yes, sir.